THE
CLOSET
PAINTERS

THE
CLOSET
PAINTERS

C. L. CARR

C.L. CARR PUBLISHING

For information contact:
carrnack8319@gmail.com

Published by:
C.L. Carr Publishing

Cover design, with assist from MidJourney,
by BlesseD'Signs @_.augustosilva._

Interior book design by Francine Platt, Eden Graphics, Inc.

This book is a work of fiction. Names, characters, places, and incidents
are the product of the author's imagination or are used fictitiously.
Any resemblance to actual events, locales, or persons, living or dead, is coincidental.

Paperback ISBN 979-8-89454-006-1

eBook ISBN 979-8-89454-007-8

Audiobook ISBN 979-8-89454-008-5

Library of Congress Control Number: 2024911003

Manufactured in the United States of America

First Edition

To Scott, John and Richard

*For all the Joy, Love, and Excitement
you bring into my life, I thank you from
the bottom of my heart. You bring me
happiness every time I think of you and
our life together!*

I SHOULDN'T BE AFRAID. I should not be angry, nor should I be thinking of how I could get rid of certain people, but that is exactly where my mind is right now.

My name is Jackson Madison. I have been in therapy for the last eight months. It seems like I would have my life straightened out by now, but I don't. Chloe, my ex-wife, was an abuser, and I was embarrassed by the fact I could not control the situation. She kept apologizing, and I kept taking her back; even though my therapist warned me against it each time I considered letting her return.

Long black hair and striking blue eyes, Chloe's physical attributes are hard to resist. A model with an athletic body, she can easily turn heads. Chloe has the uncanny ability to be loving and kind, but her quick temper dispels all attraction in the moment; she is easily provoked and comes out fighting.

I did love the person I married five years ago, but she is no longer that person. Or maybe she is, and I just failed to believe what my mind and body were telling me. However, she had a hold on me I was unable to break.

It's been a long road to recovery, and even though I still have crazy thoughts every once in a while, my life is starting to resemble normalcy, which I haven't had since I was a kid, thanks to my psychiatrist and a lot of people helping me get to this point. But it took me a long time and a lot of heartache before I was able to take my life back.

When I first got married, I thought we had a perfect life. We had fun together, laughed, spent weekends taking walks, and going out dancing and doing anything she wanted to do.

Looking back, I don't remember her ever asking me what I wanted to do which according to my therapist was a red flag. One of the many I missed or hid because I did not want to deal with any conflict between us.

I'm told I am a very talented artist, but I kept most of my art hidden. I would paint on closet walls, kitchen cabinets, and paint on the bottom of the drawers in the kitchen and then return them to their rightful place in the cabinet. I did have an art studio at home, but if I painted on canvas or in a sketchbook, I would come home from work to find the canvas slashed or my sketchbooks ripped apart.

When I asked her why she destroyed my art, she would tell me, "Because it is trash. You need to stick to flyers and promotional brochures like you do at work. Quit trying to be Picasso. You are never going to be good enough to sell anything."

ON ONE OF MY MANY TRIPS to the hospital, I was introduced to Melody. Once again, I was here with injuries caused by my wife. Melody became my therapist and psychiatrist and talked me into joining her Art Therapy Class. I didn't think I needed therapy, but it was an art class, so I was all in. Maybe I could make some art that would not be destroyed as soon as I completed a project. I was in heaven just thinking about it, and when I got home, I told my wife about it.

"How could you possibly go to an art class without checking with me first?" she spat.

"Why would you care if I did?" I replied.

She glared at me. "It's a hospital, so they will start asking questions about your accidental injuries."

I just stared at her and walked out of the room. But I did begin to regret my decision, so I called Melody the next day and told her I would not be joining the class.

Big mistake.

Three weeks later, I was back in the hospital with a broken arm from a fall. Chloe had been chasing me with a baseball bat. When she swung it at me, I ducked and fell over a stool. But she still managed to hit my shoulder as I crashed down on my arm. It was broken in two places, and surgery was required to put it back together.

When I woke from the surgery, Melody was standing at my bedside in the recovery room. She shook her head. "Next time she might kill you."

I ignored her statement. "Where is she?"

"In the waiting room. She is not permitted in the recovery room, so we can talk in private for a little while. I was not kidding about her killing you. When are you going to realize you are in real danger?"

"I know you're right, but I don't know what to do about it."

"Let's start by getting you in therapy. Then you can start the Art Therapy Class. It will be a big step and hopefully help you understand your life."

Tears filled my eyes, but I just nodded, and I decided to do what Melody was asking of me. A sense of relief came over me once I made the decision.

I didn't realize at the time, but it would turn out to be the smartest thing I've done in a long time.

ABOUT THREE WEEKS into my Art Therapy Class, Celeste joined our group. She sat in the only empty chair between me and Melody.

She gave me an odd look and turned to Melody. "What is he doing here?"

"He's new, he just joined a few weeks ago," said Melody.

"I won't have anything to say as long as he's here," Celeste whispered. Melody furrowed her brow. "Why?"

"Men are the problem."

"No, violence against a victim is the problem. Not sex, religion, or any other issue. Just be patient, he is just as much a victim as you are." She turned to me. "Jackson, this is Celeste."

I reached to shake hands with Celeste, but she immediately turned away. I turned to talk to the other students in the class.

Melody began explaining the Art Therapy lesson of the day, but she paused and asked, "Celeste, have you ever been interested in art before?"

Celeste shrugged. "Just when I was in school. It was my

favorite subject, but now that I'm older, I don't get to enjoy that any longer."

"Why not?" asked Melody.

"Because I'm too old, plus I'm no good at it. Besides, Hank would never allow me to do art."

"What do you mean he wouldn't let you?"

"He thinks I'm stupid. He says I'm not good enough to paint or draw. He's told me that before." It was time to start class. Melody didn't respond to Celeste but opened the class by having everyone introduce themselves.

Everyone briefly told why they were in class. It ranged from wanting to uncover their creativity, to escaping from reality.

Once the introductions were completed, Melody asked if anyone would like to tell their story. She said, "Sharing with others, people may realize they are not alone and that others are going through the same turmoil and fear. It can help release stress that has built up in your body."

Everyone sat in silence, so I stood up and started telling my story.

"I have always rationalized why my wife hits me, that throwing things was her way of releasing anger. She was like that even before I married her. I was taught to never hit a woman and would just back away and let her anger pass. The violence worsened after we were married, and many times I ended up in the hospital needing stitches or with broken bones.

"I consistently made up lies about how I got hurt. At the hospital, Chloe acted like the caring dutiful wife, and I convinced myself I wouldn't take it anymore. But then she would apologize, by being sweet and loving for the next several weeks, so I would be assured that all would be okay this time. I thought I truly loved her, but looking back, it was just fear that kept me there."

Celeste seemed to hang on to every word I said. Maybe my statements were mirroring things in her own life.

After I finished and sat down, Melody brought out her lesson book and started talking to the group.

"Each of us buries fears and doubts of what we cannot do," Melody said. "We all need to find an outlet to release some of the stressors in our lives. Painting, drawing, writing; all these release internal blocks and allow us to focus on those problems. You may also find answers or solutions.

"The papers, paints, and colored pencils in front of you are yours. You can scribble, draw, paint, write poetry or a story. You can also write your inner self asking questions or paint how you feel. There is no right or wrong way. There is no bad drawing, writing, or painting. This is your work, your release. Big blobs of paint on paper are acceptable if they symbolize the areas of hurt, anger, or fear in you; do what you want without fear of criticism. You have forty-five minutes to allow yourself to escape, or possibly to heal. If you have questions or need help in any way, please ask me or one of your fellow cohorts."

Melody walked away and started drawing on the board.

We were all silent; for a few minutes, you could literally hear a pin drop. Then almost at the same time, papers shuffled, colored pencils hit the table when they were dumped from boxes, and paints were squirted onto paper plates.

Melody turned back toward the class, and I noticed we were all engaging, except Celeste.

She was sitting with her arms crossed.

Melody continued drawing on her board but said, "If anyone would like to copy what I'm doing, please feel free to do so. And if you would like instructions on a certain type of creative venue, please see me after class. Everyone must put something on their paper while in class today; you must participate."

Celeste scowled and started to scribble on her paper.

When class was over, Melody advised us to leave our creative projects on our desks, and she would make sure they were put away properly.

After most of the students left, Melody walked around looking at each project, taking notes, and observing each piece.

Celeste's piece was just markings with a pencil, but when she stopped and backed away from it, there was definitely some type of form.

"Interesting," said Melody out loud.

I tried to talk to Celeste after class, but she took off running out the door. I just shook my head and wondered what I could do to help her heal. She had bruises all over her face and arms, and a black eye from a week or so ago that had already started to heal, but the internal scars would take longer to mend. I know because I was still going through the same internal turmoil that Celeste was experiencing.

Most people don't know that men are abuse victims. Maybe Celeste needs to hear more about that piece of information. Maybe then she could trust me. We could be friends possibly, so I can try and help her through her recovery.

CHAPTER 3

T HE NEXT DAY during Art Therapy, Melody again asked, "Is there anyone willing to share their story with the group?" After a few minutes of silence, I raised my hand again.

"Jackson, you have the floor," Melody said with a smile on her face as she took a seat. "I think it will help the group to hear your entire story."

"Melody has taught me that even though it is still tough to talk about, healing begins with sharing. I know a lot of you question why I am in this group. I am going to tell you, so you do not have to wonder any longer. I am an abuse victim just like you. I have never hit a woman. So, when my wife, at the time, began hitting me, I would just push her away and tell her to stop. That action would curb the behavior for a couple of days, and then as soon as she got mad at someone or something, she would take it out on me."

A woman said, "Why did you take it?"

"At first, she would just slap, but after a while, she started picking up whatever was in her reach and hit me leaving bruises, and sometimes cuts. Later, it was broken bones and stitches.

"After the third time I was in for stitches—twenty-four to be exact—the doctor in the emergency room became concerned and called Melody, to check on me and see if she could find the reasons for all my emergency room visits. Looking back, I realize it was one of the best days of my life.

"Chloe told the medics I had fallen and hit my head on the counter. Because she had hit me with a meat clever, there was blood everywhere, and I was left unconscious. She didn't call for help immediately because she needed time—about twenty-five minutes to be exact—while she cleaned up the weapon. So, they had no reason to question her story.

"The medic tried to keep me awake in case I had a concussion and drifted in and out of consciousness on the way to the hospital. When I arrived at the hospital, I was lucky enough to have the same doctor that previously treated me for my broken arm, and the suspicions immediately started again.

"Every time he asked a question, Chloe quickly answered before I could say anything. At one point, the doctor told my wife she would have to go to the waiting area because they were taking me for some tests.

"He then called Melody, who didn't wait until I was back in my room. She came right into the room where the technicians were reading the results of the test.

"'I'm here. Your wife is not permitted back in this testing area, but I understand she answered most of the questions during the admission process.' Melody frowned. 'How long are you going to continue to take this abuse?'

"I didn't answer her question, instead I asked, 'What are you talking about?'

"'Don't give me that bullshit,' she snapped, 'I know abuse when I see it and so do the doctors in this hospital. That's why they paged me; next time she might just kill you.'

"I started to cry. I'm not sure if it was because my head hurt so bad or if it was the fact I was relieved that someone actually knew what was going on and did not judge me."

CHAPTER 4

I WAS LEFT WITH PRESSURE on my brain, so I was off work for several weeks. Even though I was determined to do something about Chloe and the abuse, I let her back in. She was so loving and took such good care of me and promised it would never happen again. She seemed so sincere.

Another big mistake!

I went back to work, and the abuse started all over again. When I brought up her promise of no more violence, she laughed, walked out the door to go to work, and it slammed behind her. It ate at me so bad, that when I got to work, I decided to call Melody and make an appointment.

By the time I got to the door of Melody's office, I had already talked myself out of going in. I rationalized I was overreacting, maybe Chloe was having a bad day, maybe I was provoking her in some way without realizing it.

So, I left.

The bright sun felt so good, I just stood and basked in its warmth for a few minutes. The sun caused my eyes to be a little blurry. I was able to focus when I started back to my car, and what I saw next shocked and infuriated me.

In the next parking lot, I saw Chloe passionately kissing another man.

The two of them got in the car, and they drove away. I wrote down the license number. I reached to open my car door when I heard someone call my name. I ignored it, got in my car, and drove to work.

When I got home that night, Chloe had dinner on the table. She had poured two glasses of wine, and candles were lit. She ran up and kissed me and threw her arms around my neck.

I backed away to catch my breath.

Was I mistaken today? Maybe it wasn't her. I decided to go along with her for the evening and see where it went. We talked about our day and plans for the weekend to go hiking in the mountains. We finished our wine and went to bed. The sex was fantastic, as usual.

I tried to process what I saw today but decided I must have been mistaken because the night was so beautiful.

The next morning, I decided to go the long way driving by Melody's office just to see if maybe I could find the person I saw yesterday.

I pulled into the parking lot and waited. I gave myself fifteen minutes. If nothing happened by then, I would go on to work. Seven minutes passed, and I saw Chloe drive into the parking lot and get out of her car. The same man I saw her with yesterday ran right up to her, grabbed her, and they kissed—just like the day before.

I lost it. I backed my car out of the parking space, stepped on the gas heading straight toward them as they stood in the middle of the parking lot kissing and touching each other.

They both screamed and jumped back. I slammed on the brakes, jumped out of my car, and started toward them.

"What the hell do you think you are doing?" Chloe screamed. "Didn't I give you enough last night?"

The man snarled. "Who is that?"

"My husband."

"Oh, he's the one," the man chuckled.

She nodded. "Yes."

"Now I know why you need an outlet. He's crazy," the man laughed.

I demanded, "Who are you?"

Chloe smiled. "Just a friend." The man laughed.

"Really? People don't usually kiss a friend that way."

"There's no reason to get angry, Jackson. Just go home, and I'll see you tonight."

"No, you will not see me tonight. We are over! I'll pack your things, and you can pick them up tomorrow."

Chloe became irate, swinging her purse at me, and hitting me with her fists. I tried to hold her back, but she jumped on me and slammed her keys into my face. We both fell backward onto the blacktop; I tried to push her off me, but she just kept hammering me with her fists.

Finally, the friend pulled her off me.

He looked stunned. "What the hell? What's going on?"

Chloe got up and brushed herself off. Blood was running down her leg, but she ignored it. She glared at me but answered her friend, "Nothing."

"Nothing? What is that supposed to mean? You're acting like a crazy woman, and you want me to think everything is okay? Is that what you think? It's not going to happen."

He turned and walked away.

She hurried after him, so I got in my car and left.

CHAPTER 5

I THOUGHT ABOUT CALLING MELODY, but I didn't know what to say to her.

My wife beats me up.

Sounds so lame.

Instead, I decided to let sleeping dogs lie, as they say. Probably wasn't the smartest thing I have ever done, but how could I explain what was happening in my life that anyone would understand?

When I got home, I packed her clothes and shoes and left them in the hallway. I figured we could decide later on the rest of the household items who gets what.

By the time I took a shower and got dressed, it was already noon. I went to the diner to grab lunch before going to work. While I was eating, Melody came in, and when she saw me, walked directly to my table.

"You missed your appointment," she said flatly. "I know. Something came up."

"Fear?"

"No, it wasn't fear. I just thought I had worked things out, so I didn't need your help."

"And did your way work?"

"Not really." I looked down at the table. I didn't want her to see how much I was hurting.

"I'm free tomorrow afternoon at two. Come in and we can talk. If what I say doesn't help or make sense, don't come back."

"I'll think about it."

She started to leave but turned around. "Nothing will ever change without therapy, but something drastic usually happens before they are ready, or forced to get help."

"What do you mean, forced to get help?"

"Someone is critically injured or killed." She turned on her heel and left.

I guess that could happen to me. No, deep down I know she truly loves me.

CHAPTER 6

I DIDN'T HEAR from Chloe that day.

When I woke up the following morning, I was surprised how good it felt to get up, shower, have breakfast, and read the newspaper without interruptions. I decided to keep my appointment with Melody.

It couldn't hurt to listen to what she has to say.

Maybe she could give me some tips on how to handle my wife when she gets angry, so I can try to defuse the situation before it gets out of hand. I should be able to handle this myself, but a few pointers may help.

At 1:30 p.m., I was trying to talk myself out of the meeting with Melody, but I was determined to hear her out, so at 1:55 p.m., I was standing in her office. She seemed surprised to see me.

She smiled. "Have a seat wherever you feel most comfortable."

Her office walls were lined with furniture, but some were set in cozy corners. I chose the one next to the fireplace with big poofy pillows.

Melody picked up her pen and tablet. "You can sit or lie

down, whatever you prefer."

I felt comfortable and safe, and I started talking before she sat down. I felt like someone had unplugged my mouth. I was saying things I never shared with anyone before. I must have talked nonstop for an hour and fifteen minutes without hardly taking a breath.

The next thing I remember is waking up feeling extremely refreshed. I looked around, sat up, and realized I had been asleep for over two hours. I stood and stretched, then looked around for Melody. She was sitting at her desk on the other side of the room.

"Welcome back," she said with a chuckle. "I hope you didn't have to be anywhere this afternoon."

I felt my face flush. "I'm so sorry."

"You have nothing to be sorry for. You did exactly what was needed; released pent up anger, frustration, and tension. Your body completely relaxed probably for the first time in a long while, so, you slept."

"But I didn't get to hear anything you had to say."

"I can tell you right now if you like. First, you are in real danger. It's not *if, but when. Abusers don't stop for any reason other* than when they go too far and someone steps in. Usually, the abused is too terrified to make the move, so it is left up to the police, hospital, or someone else outside the situation to notify local authorities. I know right now you are feeling better, and probably more confident, than you have in a long time, so you think you can handle anything. Because you're a man, it's even worse, but it doesn't work that way."

I nodded. I knew she was right.

"Abusers don't care about the sex of their abusee. They just see a vulnerable person, and they take advantage of them."

I nodded again.

She looked at me for a few seconds then asked, "Can we make your next appointment?"

"Yes."

"Okay, this is Tuesday, how about Friday at two?"

"Could we make it three? That way I can go home afterward instead of going back to work."

"Great. Three o'clock Friday it is."

I left her office feeling light, without burdens. I guess I never realized just how stressed I had become. I stopped and picked up takeout for dinner and went home.

WE NEED TO TALK was plastered on my front door.

I crumbled the note, sat down in front of the TV, and ate my dinner. The evening was very quiet and peaceful. While watching TV, I realized I could do some painting without worry of it being destroyed. So, I made my way back to my studio, set things up in the closet, and started to paint in the closet.

Wait! Don't have to paint in the closet, I can paint on canvas. The joy that flooded my body was unbelievable. I painted until about one in the morning. I cannot describe the feeling of joy I felt while I was painting.

I had put my phone on mute when I was in Melody's office and forgot to take it off, so when I picked it up to set the alarm, I noticed five missed calls and three messages, all from Chloe.

I didn't want to lose the peacefulness I was feeling, so I decided not to look at the messages or return the calls until morning.

Even though I had slept for two hours that afternoon, I fell asleep easily.

I MISSED MY FRIDAY APPOINTMENT with Melody. She left me a message saying she knew Fridays were bad for me, so she rescheduled my appointment for Tuesday at three o'clock.

That was good for me, so I texted her to let her know I would be there.

I had not heard anything from Chloe, and my life, for the first time in what seemed like forever, was very peaceful. I was productive on my job, getting more work completed. My creativity was back, and my mind was flowing with new ideas. Things were going well, so that Tuesday I called and canceled my appointment.

I saw Melody's number on my phone, but I answered it anyway. "Hey, Melody."

"You know why I'm calling, Jackson. I'd like you to reconsider coming in for your appointment."

"Things are going great in my life now; I don't think I need any therapy. I haven't heard from my wife in over two weeks, so things are good."

"Be careful, Jackson," said Melody. "Keep your guard up." But of course, I ignored her warning.

Another week went by, and I was getting used to my emotional freedom. Being alone sixteen hours a day seven days a week, I started to realize how much I was bottling up inside. But I spent eight hours a day with people, and that was pleasant, too. My work improved to the point I was impressing even myself, and my colleagues noticed; so did my boss.

I had not realized just how messed up my life had been until it began to unfold into this beautiful life of bliss, that I can't ever remember having any time in my life. How could I have not seen what was happening to me? Why did I not feel the heaviness of my emotions until now, when suddenly they seemed light?

I thought about that for a while trying to pinpoint times when I should have noticed and done something about my emotional state. But I stopped thinking about it when I realized it was taking away the joy and peace I was feeling now.

I made myself a promise I would not let anyone, or anything, interfere with my glorious state of being I was experiencing.

I went to bed, but I woke in the middle of the night with a feeling of dread. I adjusted my pillow, wondering if it had been a bad dream that caused me to feel this way. Dark depression is the only way I can explain the intense discomfort I was feeling, my peace and joy were gone.

I decided to get up, so I turned over in my bed.

"If I can't have you, no one can!" Chloe screamed and sank a knife into my groin.

The pain was excruciating. I rolled out of bed to get away from her. When I hit the floor, she raised the knife and flung herself at me again.

I grabbed her hair and pulled her down to the floor, but she managed to slash my arm.

Blood spurted everywhere. I felt like I was going to pass out, so I grabbed her arm and gave one more pull to stop her. Her scream was deafening. I knew I had cut her.

I was fading out of consciousness, and I thought I heard someone else in the apartment. I saw the image of a man standing over me, but I knew I was dying.

CHAPTER 8

I DRIFTED IN AND OUT of consciousness, but I couldn't stay awake. When I finally did, I learned I had been in the hospital for five days.

"Well, Mr. Madison, how are you feeling?" A short curly haired nurse grinned at me.

I didn't answer, but she added, "You have some visitors."

Melody came into my room along with two police officers. I was not only in pain but confused. "What's going on?"

"The police are here to get your story if you feel up to it," said Melody.

"My story." I tried to sit up.

Monitors went off, and the doctor came running into my room. My blood pressure and heart rate had shot up, and the doctor dismissed the police.

As soon as I relaxed, my heart rate and blood pressure regulated.

The doctor wanted me to go back to sleep, so Melody said she would be back later.

I woke up thirsty and groggy at four o'clock in the afternoon. I tried to find the nurse call button, but again, as soon as I tried to sit up, the monitors started buzzing.

"Well, I guess that's one way to call for a doctor or nurse," I said as they both rushed into my room.

"At least he has his sense of humor back." The doctor laughed and checked my heart and blood pressure.

"Is this going to happen every time I move?"

"We are not quite sure why this is happening when you move, but it's not a good sign. We're going to monitor you over the next couple of days to see if we can get you stabilized."

"See if what stabilizes?"

"Your body has been through a traumatic event. You've had three surgeries in four days, it will take a while to heal. But evidently, something is telling us you need to lay still and stay calm for a few more days. We need to figure out why that is."

"I've been here five days. What day is this?" The nurse smiled. "It's Tuesday."

"I've been here since Friday?"

"Yes."

"Wow!" I shouted.

I can't believe that came out of my mouth. "What kind of surgeries?"

The doctor asked, "Do you remember what happened to put you here?"

"Yes, my wife stabbed me." I clearly remembered the horrible night.

"Well, she did a great job of it. You had injuries to your groin, blood vessels slashed in your arm, and a punctured intestine, not to mention a concussion from hitting your head on something."

"Wow. I'm sorry for saying that again, but it is all starting to come back to me now."

Again, the monitors went off, and the doctor refused to discuss any more. He told the nurse to schedule me for an MRI and CAT scan for the next day, and I was to be on total bed rest with no visitors until then.

What is going on?

I was so tired I just drifted off to sleep. I slept all night, waking only when they came in to get me for the scans the next day.

The scans showed bleeding in my stomach, so back to surgery I went for the fourth time.

CHAPTER 9

WHEN I WOKE UP this time, I felt a lot better, and did not feel as weak. I actually could sit up in bed without the monitors blaring.

When they brought my lunch, it consisted of broth, Sprite, and Jell-O. Even though I couldn't eat much, I was grateful for the food.

Over the next few days, I slowly started to get a little of my strength back. It was about that time the police returned. They started asking questions about the night I was stabbed. After I finished my rendition of the story, the police told me Chloe had filed charges against me for assault and battery.

I could not believe what I was hearing.

"Filing charges against me? She broke into my apartment in the middle of the night and stabbed me in the groin. I told you what happened."

"You're saying she attacked you, right?" one police officer asked.

"Yes."

"Her version of the story is quite different."

"Really, how so?"

"She says you attacked her."

"Think about it officer. I'm the one in the hospital having surgeries, four to be exact. Now she's walking around perfectly healthy, but I attacked her. Is that what you are telling me?"

"She had surgery also. She has a face full of stitches. She was sliced from her ear down to her mouth."

"Maybe the guy that was with her sliced her face."

"She says there was no one else in the apartment except you and her," the same officer said.

"She's lying."

At that moment, Melody walked into my room.

"Gentlemen," she said to the police officers, "do you have your statement?"

"Yes," one of them answered, but they both nodded.

"Then you will please excuse us. It's time for Jackson's therapy."

They both thanked me, and one of them said, "We'll be in touch, Mr. Madison."

I was irritated and stared out the window. "Okay," I said without looking up. Then I asked, "Melody, what's going on?"

"Your wife is trying to pin attempted murder on you."

I was stunned. "How can they possibly believe that?" I stared at her with my mouth hanging open.

CHAPTER 10

AFTER TWO OR THREE WEEKS of surgeries, I was in therapy off and on all day for the next seven days. They would let me rest in between sessions, and then I was back at it again. Each day I was getting stronger, so I kept working hard to recover.

On the eighth day, I was so excited when the doctor reported I would be discharged the following day but would have to continue the therapy for a few more weeks on an outpatient basis.

However, the next morning was not a great day for me. As I was signing all the discharged papers, the police showed up and arrested me for attempted murder. My wife had succeeded in convincing the police I was the instigator of the fiasco.

Frustrated and angry, I sat in the jail cell wondering what to do next. The bailiff came to my rescue by announcing that my attorney was here to see me.

"I didn't know I had an attorney."

"Well, you do." He escorted me to a room with no windows, a table, and two chairs.

In walked a tall handsome man in a tailored suit and glossy shiny shoes. He introduced himself as Attorney Peter Sabastin. I had heard of him but had never met him.

"How are you today?"

"I could be better."

"Yes, I can see that," he stated. "You are about to be released. Your bail is being paid as we speak."

What a relief I felt after he made that statement, but I was still confused. "Who is paying my bail and who got you for my attorney?"

"We'll discuss that later. Right now, we have a little time for you to tell me what really happened."

I told him the entire story with all the gory details, and then I threw my hands up in the air and screamed, "I don't know how this is all happening!"

"Take a deep breath and calm down. I'm going to take care of this.

"Your wife has thirty-eight stitches in her face and claims you attacked her. I got a copy of her statement before I came over to talk to you. You said there was another man in the room? She says there was no one except you and her. Do you know who else was there? Can you describe him?"

"No and no."

"But you are sure there was another person in the apartment?"

"Yes, I'm very sure."

We went over more details for about fifteen minutes longer before the bailiff announced I had been released.

"Go home, relax, and I'll call you after I do some more

work on your case. I'm thinking we could meet after lunch tomorrow, around one o'clock. Will that work for you?"

"Yes, but I need to know why you're doing this for me. Who hired you?"

"Melody. I believe she's your therapist slash psychiatrist, correct?"

"Why would she do that?"

He grinned. "She's my wife. I'm Peter." That made me smile, too.

"C'mon, I will give you a ride home."

CHAPTER 11

ON THE WAY HOME, Peter said, "You are to have no contact with your wife for any reason until the trial. If she contacts you in any way; letters, notes, phone, or comes to your home, you are to contact the police immediately, and then call me.

"If anyone else contacts you about the case, call me right away. Do not try to handle anything yourself because you may make matters worse. Since she is lying about the attack, she will lie about everything else. Be safe and let me do my job. We can win this."

When he dropped me off at home, I felt much better. However, that feeling was short lived. When I walked into my apartment it had been ransacked. Not just the bedroom where the fight took place, but the entire apartment had been demolished.

There was a knock on my door. I froze. "Jackson, it's Peter Sabastin." Relieved, I opened the door.

"I remember you had not been here since it all happened, so I thought you might need a little support," he said.

"Thanks, I'm in total shock. So, this happened after the

fight in the bedroom," I asked as I was pointing to the destruction. Police tape was still on the bedroom door, but the rest of my house was just rubble like an earthquake had hit.

Mr. Sabastin called the police and asked for officers to be dispatched to the apartment.

They arrived shortly and were surprised to see the mess that happened while I was gone.

My attorney assured me this would help with my case since we could prove I was in the hospital the entire time until I was taken to jail, so someone other than me did the damage. He then stepped out into the hall to take a phone call.

I sat on a chair in amazement. I knew this had to be Chloe. No one else would ever consider doing this to me.

Mr. Sabastin came back into the room and said, "Melody has a small apartment for you to stay in for the next few days until we can get your home cleaned up."

"No, I think I will just stay here and start cleaning it myself. It will keep me busy and my mind off this nightmare I am living in right now, but thanks."

"Are you sure?"

"Yes, right now I just want to be alone."

"Okay." He laid his business card on the kitchen counter. "Call me any time. Both my phone numbers are on the card. Otherwise, I will see you tomorrow at one."

"Okay, tomorrow at one," I mumbled.

CHAPTER 12

I STARTED FILLING TRASH BAGS with all the debris. It wasn't as bad as it looked. Broken glass everywhere, and cushions tossed across the room, and furniture turned upside down. I could clean and throw away what was destroyed because police had pictures of everything.

I had worked in the apartment for about an hour when there was a knock on the door. I froze.

My attorney told me I was to have no contact with my wife, and I couldn't think of anyone else who would be at my door. I just stood there in the middle of my bedroom hoping they would leave.

From outside, I heard, "Jackson, it's Melody."

I relaxed and opened the door. She was standing there with two other people.

"We came to help you clean up, Jackson. Peter told me what a mess you came home to.

Can we come in?"

I didn't answer immediately. When the silence got uncomfortable, I finally said, "Sure." I stepped aside, and they walked in.

Melody motioned to me. "This is Jackson—Jackson, meet Abby and Caroline."

I nodded. "Nice to meet you."

Everyone immediately jumped in, picking up trash and started sweeping broken glass. I walked back to the bedroom where I was ready to wash down the walls and furniture to remove blood stains. Melody followed me. She looked around and then ask, "Do you have any coffee?"

"Yes, would you like a cup?"

She laughed. "Yes, I would. I work better with coffee at my side."

"I'll go make us a pot."

"Let me have your sponge, and I will work on the walls while you make coffee and rest for a few minutes. You looked exhausted."

"I am, it's been a long week."

By the time the coffee was done, Melody had rolled up the blood-stained rug and finished wiping up blood on the wall and nightstand. The rest of Melody's crew had turned the furniture back over, fluffed the cushions, and was in the process of sweeping the floors and vacuuming the furniture. My place was starting to look normal again.

They hauled the many bags of trash out to the dumpster and then told Melody they were leaving. I thanked them as did Melody, and we sat back drinking our coffee.

"Thank you so much for all you did, Melody." She smiled. "You're welcome, it's my pleasure." I sighed. "What now."

"Peter will be able to give you more details, but they will probably set a court date sometime next week. Depending on what happens then, Peter will let you know where you'll go from there."

After we finished our coffee, Melody said, "Your wife's attorney is trying for attempted murder charges."

My blood boiled. "I just can't believe that."

"Well believe it," Melody said. "Because she is out to get you at any cost."

"But why? What did I do to deserve this?"

"She's a model, has thirty-eight stitches across her face, and she's a narcissist. She is angrier now than she was before all this happened. She will do anything to make this your fault, so be careful what you say and who you say it to. Remember, no contact with her. NONE."

"I know. Peter told me the same thing."

We talked for the next couple of hours, and she asked about the pictures painted inside the closet she had discovered while cleaning. I explained to her I had to paint inside of closets, bottoms of drawers, anywhere that could be hidden because if I painted on canvas, Chloe destroyed them.

"That is so sad." She sighed. "You look really tired, Jackson, I'm going to go and let you get some rest."

We walked toward the door but stopped when someone started beating on my door. Melody shoved me away from the door. "Get in the bedroom. NOW!"

I was so startled I did exactly what she told me to do. I shut my bedroom door and put my ear against it so I could hear. Melody opened the front door.

I heard her say, "May I help you?"

"Who are you?"

It was Chloe.

"Who are you and what do you want?" Melody asked without answering the previous question.

"I'm Jackson's wife and I want to talk to him," Chloe snapped.

"No, you will not talk to him," Melody said. "You are not to be anywhere around him so please leave or I will call the police."

Chloe's voice shot up an octave. "Go ahead and call the police. He's going to pay for what he did to me."

Melody must have called because I heard her give the police the address, and then she said, "Get out, the police are on their way."

I knew if I went out there, it would be a bad idea, so I just stood by the door listening, in case Melody needed me.

"Is he here?" Chloe demanded.

Melody answered, "Yes, but he is sleeping."

"Who are you?"

"I am his doctor…" Melody barely got the words out when I heard sirens, then a knock on the bedroom door.

"You can come out now."

I opened the door. "Did she leave?"

Melody chuckled. "Yep, when she heard the sirens, she took off down the stairs."

THE NEXT DAY, Peter called to say we had a court date on Wednesday which was two days from now. He had obtained the complaint and needed to talk to me prior to us going to court.

When we met, he told me what to expect. He said my wife had filed an abuse claim and said I assaulted her. He also told me when we got to court, I would have to make a plea. He suggested a *Not Guilty plea.* So, when we got to court on Wednesday, that's exactly what I did.

The judge set a trial date for April 28 at nine o'clock am. That was the first time I had seen Chloe since the night of the attack. Her face was swollen, and she had stitches from her left eye down to her lip.

I immediately started to feel sorry for her.

Peter jolted me back to reality. "I can see by that look, Jackson, you are feeling bad for her. Snap out of it. She tried to kill you."

I took a deep breath and nodded in agreement.

I was able to go home because they still had the bail money that was paid to get me out of jail after I was arrested.

I knew Melody and Peter had something to do with that, I just didn't know what yet.

Over the next few days, I didn't know why, but I wanted to work, so I went back to my job. I also restarted my sessions with Melody. Between the two, I was able to keep my mind occupied with positives instead of worrying about what might happen.

In our sessions, Melody taught me I didn't do anything to deserve the treatment I received from Chloe. She also assured me I was not less of a man because I put up with the abuse so long. She made me realize I could fully recover from what was happening.

"I honestly thought I could fix things with her, though."

"That's a normal reaction for men that are in abusive relationships. The problem with that mindset is, the abuser knows that. Therefore, they abuse and then play on emotions by apologizing and saying it will never happen again. They become loving and attentive for the next few days or weeks before their anger rears its ugly head again. Without help, it's just a viscous cycle that keeps going round and round. The abuse usually gets more and more violent with each passing episode."

CHAPTER 14

I MARKED THE DAYS off on the calendar as we got closer to the court date. Now it's here, and it all comes to a head.

Will she really stick by her story and pretend that I was the aggressor?

Court was just like it is on TV. I was glad I had watched several courtroom programs because for some reason, it calmed my nerves somewhat. Peter was right by my side, and Melody was in the courtroom, also.

When the prosecutor questioned my wife, I could not believe the accusations that were coming out of her mouth. She had concocted a story out of a horror film, and not one word of it was true. She never looked at me once when she was on the stand telling her story.

I tightened my hand into a fist, and Peter just patted my arm. He watched me, and I understood what that pat meant, because he had made it clear to me, we can't let the judge see any anger or hostility on our side, or he may conclude my wife was correct in her accusations.

Chloe's words were, "My husband is a hostile person and always ready to beat someone up over the littlest things."

Basically, what she was doing was describing her personality traits but putting them on me.

Peter was very good in his examination and caught her in lies twice. But after Peter was finished, her attorney did a cross-examination and helped her clarify her previous statements.

When I was on the stand, I was prepared for everything Peter was asking. I told the story exactly how it happened from start to finish. I felt good until her lawyer did the cross-examination.

"And you say there was another person in the apartment with your wife other than you the night of the attack," her attorney questioned.

"Yes."

"Who was the other person?"

"I don't know."

"You don't know, but you know there was someone there?"

"Yes, he was standing over me after my wife stabbed me. What happened after that I don't know because I passed out."

"You saw the man and then you passed out, am I understanding what you are saying."

"Yes."

"Couldn't it be possible that since you say you passed out that maybe what you thought you saw was a hallucination caused by the pain you say you were in?"

"No, I saw a man standing over me. She's lying."

"According to police, there were no signs of any other

person in the home. Did the other person hurt you?" he asked.

"I don't know. I passed out. All I know is he was standing over me before I lost consciousness."

"So maybe since you were fading in and out of consciousness, you could have just thought you saw someone that really wasn't there, is that possible?"

"No." I raised my voice. "I saw someone standing over me. I know I did."

"Objection," Peter stated. "This is badgering the witness."

"Sustained," said the judge.

He then asked, "Did you slice your wife's face with a knife?"

"I think so."

"Why?"

"I was trying to get the knife away from her, and when I jerked it out of her hand it accidentally cut her."

"Did you see the cut."

"No, I just heard her scream," I said. "That's when I saw the man. He came in the room and stood over me."

I guess my mind went back to that night, and I was replaying it all in my mind. I must have been so spaced out that the judge banged his gavel on his bench and called out my name.

"Yes, sir."

The judge said, "Answer the question."

I felt like an idiot, but I asked, "What question?"

Peter stood and asked the judge for a recess. "It's been a long trying morning. Could we break for lunch?"

The judge agreed and gave us two hours before we had to be back in court. We stood and Peter asked, "What do you like to eat?"

"I don't know. Could we just get something and sit in the park next to the courthouse and eat?"

"Excellent idea."

We got a sandwich from the food truck next to the park. It was very tasty, but the fresh air was more helpful than anything else.

It was a beautiful spring day, birds singing, sun shining, fluffy white clouds, and about seventy degrees.

It was a perfect day, then I remembered what was happening today. I reminded myself I could control how I feel about anything just by putting my focus on something pleasant and beautiful. So, I took a deep breath and let the sun warm my face. I closed my eyes and listened for the birds to sing their songs. It was calming and peaceful, and just what I needed before we went back into the courthouse.

The rest of the afternoon went quickly because the prosecutor asked the judge for a recess very abruptly.

Peter was confused and so was I, but it gave us a much-needed break so neither of us complained.

I WENT HOME and fixed dinner for myself and watched the Cincinnati Reds beat the LA Dodgers. I like baseball, but I don't get much time to watch it or go to any games. I root for the Reds because my family lives fifteen minutes from the stadium, and we usually go to a game or two when I go home for a visit. When I was a kid, going to the Reds games was a highlight during the summer. Once when I was watching a game on TV, I saw my brother and my nephew in the stands as the camera scanned the crowd.

I need to go back home again.

I didn't want to worry my mom and dad, so I didn't call them when I got arrested. None of my family knew what was going on in my life. I knew they would be upset when they found out, but by that time, it would be all over and everything back to normal.

Well, that's what I was hoping.

We had to be in court the next morning at ten o'clock. Peter called at eight a.m. and said we needed to meet before the trial resumed, so we met at nine.

Peter started by saying, "We need to find the guy that was in your room the night of the attack."

He seemed earnest, and I was surprised. "Why, what's going on?"

"The judge seems to be leaning toward your wife on this issue, so we need to somehow find out who that person was. Do you have any idea at all who it could be?"

"I have no clue. Like I said, I was fading in and out. I vaguely remember a shadow."

"A big, tall, short, small, what kind of a shadow?"

"I think he was wearing some type of vest, maybe a cowboy type, but I'm not real sure." I was starting to feel frustrated. "Why would the judge be leaning in her favor?"

"Because she is saying there was no one else except you and her in the apartment, and that she stabbed you, after you cut her face. She says she was fearful for her life, so she stabbed you until you couldn't get up.

"You're saying there was another man in the room, so we need to find him to collaborate your story and discredit hers.

"Think of all the people you know who might also know her. Any friends that would help her? Does she have any friends or work colleagues that might help her, or do something like this?"

I was honestly bewildered. "I don't think so."

"Keep thinking, I'm going to put out a plea on social media, asking for anyone with information about this case to come forward. We need all the help we can get, so we'll offer a reward and see what happens."

I was a little concerned at that point. Before this conversation, he was very reassuring that we had nothing to worry about, but now he seemed a little panicky.

Peter left to put the information on Facebook, and I started writing down names of people that Chloe and I know, and also names of her friends that I could remember.

When I wrote a name, I would picture that person in my mind to see if I could match an image with what I remembered seeing that night. However, after twenty-five names, I was no closer to identifying the person I saw in my bedroom.

Peter returned with his script for Facebook. He read it to me, and it sounded great. "But who is going to admit to taking part in an attempted murder charge when they don't have to?"

Peter raised his eyebrows and twisted his mouth, but he didn't respond to my question.

Peter said he wanted me to continue going over people in my mind and remember everyone I could think of that possibly could have helped her in any way. I racked my brain most of the afternoon and evening but came up with no one. So, I went to bed with a headache from thinking too much.

I woke in the middle of the night with a thought.

How did she get into my apartment that night. She didn't have a key because the locks had been changed after the police concluded their investigation. The door wasn't broken, but where would she get a key? Maybe the landlord let her in not knowing we had split up. After all, he had done that many times before for us.

Before I could call the landlord the next day, Peter called me to see if I had come up with any names. I told him no but gave him my idea of calling the landlord.

Peter said he would take care of contacting the landlord, and if I wanted to come along with him, I could, but I was not to go by myself. I was to stay out of the investigative part of the process. We left a message with the Office Assistant to have him call Peter when he returned later that day.

So, we went back to court with nothing new.

The prosecutor questioned a couple of character witnesses for Chloe then the judge asked Peter if he had any further witnesses.

Peter said, "Not at this time, but we are following a lead."

The judge told us, "You have until ten o'clock tomorrow morning to produce additional information or witnesses, otherwise we will adjourn, and I will make my decision based on current testimony."

"Yes, Your Honor," Peter replied, and the proceedings were over for the day.

CHAPTER 16

WE WALKED OUT of the courtroom, and I asked Peter, "What am I supposed to do if he rules in her favor?"

"Don't panic, we still have time. We'll find something or someone to help."

The next morning, we were back in court, and Peter seemed in a very upbeat mood.

I was curious and just as the judge entered the courtroom, I asked, "What's up?"

The bailiff addressed the courtroom, "All rise."

The judge asked, "Mr. Sabastin, do you have additional information you would like to present to this court?"

Peter stood. "Yes, judge."

"I would like to call Mr. Jonathan Breeze to the stand."

There was a rumble from the prosecutors table when that announcement was made.

As Mr. Breeze came forward and took the stand, my wife got visibly agitated, to the point the judge asked if something was wrong.

Her attorney quickly replied, "Nothing is wrong, judge."

The judge grumbled, "Then keep the noise down in my courtroom."

"Yes, judge," said her attorney.

Mr. Breeze was sworn in, and then Peter began questioning him.

"Do you know the defendant in this courtroom," Peter asked.

"Yes," Mr. Breeze answered.

"And do you know Mrs. Madison?"

"Yes."

"How do you know Mr. and Mrs. Madison?"

Mr. Breeze nodded. "They are tenants of mine."

"How long have they been tenants of yours?"

Mr. Breeze looked directly at me. "Mr. Madison has been there for five years, very good tenant."

"And Mrs. Madison?"

"She has only been around a little over a year."

I noticed he didn't look at Chloe.

"On the night of March 15, 2019, when Mr. Madison was stabbed, did you see Mrs. Madison that evening?"

"Yes, I did," said Mr. Breeze.

"Liar!" Chloe screamed and jumped to her feet.

The judge banged his gavel. "One more outburst like that, and she will be found in contempt of court."

The judge turned to Mr. Breeze. "I'm sorry Mr. Breeze, please continue."

Peter repeated the question, "Did you see Mrs. Madison on the night Mr. Madison was stabbed and if so, when?"

"Yes," said Mr. Breeze again. "Around midnight."

"Where was she when you saw her?"

"At my apartment. She banged on my door and woke me up. She said she had locked herself out of their apartment and needed me to let her in. I didn't know at the time that she and Mr. Madison had separated."

"Did you let her into the apartment?"

"Yes." He looked at me again, only this time he seemed apologetic.

Peter asked, "Mr. Breeze, can you tell us what happened next?"

"She thanked me, and I went back to my apartment and went back to sleep. A little while later, I heard sirens and got up to see what was going on. I noticed the medics were going into Mr. Madison apartment. The police came, and the ambulance left with someone. I did not know it was Mr. Madison at the time," explained Mr. Breeze.

"Thinking back to that night, was there anyone else around or with her?" asked Peter.

"Yes," Mr. Breeze answered. "There was a man with her."

"Did you know the man or ask who he was?"

"No, to both questions."

Peter then asked, "Did you actually see the man go into Mr. Madison's apartment with Mrs. Madison?"

"Yes, as I was waiting for the elevator, I turned around. Both Mrs. Madison and the man were entering the apartment."

"You are certain that both Mrs. Madison and the man, both of them, went into the apartment," Peter asked again.

"Yes, I'm positive."

"No further questions of this witness at this time."

"Any cross-examination?" the judge asked.

"Not at this time," said Chloe's attorney.

He then asked the judge for a recess which the judge granted.

We left the courtroom. Peter said he had some calls to make, so I went to the diner to get some lunch.

The break was supposed to be two hours; however, Peter called me and said the judge had a request for the rest of the day off from Chloe's attorney, and the judge had granted it.

Peter told me, "Evidently, her attorney didn't know about the other man until it was brought out in court today, so I'm sure they are having a heated discussion this afternoon. He will have to rethink his approach to defending her, and that's hard to do once you find out your client has lied to you. You start to question everything they previously told you."

CHAPTER 17

WE WALKED TO OUR CARS, and Peter said, "That was a brilliant idea to check with your landlord to see how she got into your apartment. It made the break in the case. We still haven't won yet, but the table has changed more in our favor since she was proven a liar. The judge will have to rethink his position on the case, it seems like he was leaning toward Chloe."

Peter said he would see me in court the next day at ten. He said he had some more research to do. I went back home and laid down. This entire business of going to court and not knowing what the outcome would be was really wearing me out.

I was in a deep sleep when the phone started ringing. I forced my eyes open and looked at the clock. It was five p.m. Then I looked at my phone and saw it was Chloe calling. I didn't know whether to answer or not, so I let it go to voice mail.

What could she possibly want anyway?

Peter said I was to have no contact with her, but maybe she just wants to find out how I'm doing.

We are still married after all.

I waited for a few minutes and then decided to call Peter and get his advice.

Melody answered the call.

"Did I call the wrong number?" I asked.

Melody answered, "No, Peter just went out to his car to get his briefcase. Are you okay?"

"Chloe just tried to call me, but I didn't answer. I was just going to check with Peter to see if I should call her back."

"I can answer that question for you. No, you are not to have any contact with her outside of the courtroom. Do not let her pull you into her drama."

Peter must have walked back into the house because Melody was telling him I was on the phone and why.

Peter got on the phone and said, "This is a ploy on her part to try and make you feel sorry for her. Do not go there. Just let it keep going to voice mail but do not erase them. They will come in handy when we are in court since she has been told she is to have no contact with you. Also, as vicious as she is, she could be trying to set you up to get things turned back around in her favor. Right now, she has lost her creditability."

"Okay," I said. "I will see you in court tomorrow. Sorry to have bothered you."

Peter said, "Jackson, you are never a bother. Call any time you have questions or just need to talk."

"Thanks, Peter." I pushed end on my phone.

I was still very curious about what she wanted, but I did as I was told and let it go to voice mail all six times she called.

Then it occurred to me that since I did not answer the phone, she may come over to my house again. I decided to go into work for a little while to take my mind off the entire mess. I knew she wouldn't come to my work because she didn't like my coworkers, and they did not care for her, either.

I was relieved to see friendly, supportive faces when I entered my workspace.

Jewel was a coworker. "Hey, I thought you were in court today," she said.

"I was, but they recessed early, and I needed a change of scenery, so I decided to work for a little while."

Jack, another coworker, said, "It's good to see you."

"We have all missed you," Jewel grinned.

Feeling a little emotional I simply said, "Thanks."

I worked after everyone else left, well into the evening. It felt great. I sat back in my chair and read over the work I had completed. It was a beautiful evening, and I had not felt this good in a really long time. I like my job and the work that I do. I guess I had forgotten that little detail. I left about eight thirty, stopped at the drive through and picked up a sandwich, then I went home.

CHAPTER 18

THE NEXT MORNING as I was pulling out of the driveway, I saw Chloe. She was sitting in her car across the street. I hurried and backed out the opposite way her car was facing, so it would not be easy for her to follow me. I picked up my phone and called Peter, but I watched her in the rearview mirror trying to navigate turning around in traffic.

Peter answered, and I told him about her being in front of my house this morning.

"Go directly to the courthouse. I am on my way," Peter said.

Before I could hang up the phone, Chloe rammed the back of my car.

I yelled; it might have been a scream. Whatever, it scared me to death.

Peter yelled through the phone, "What's going on?"

"She just rammed the back of my car!"

"I'll meet you at the courthouse." The phone went dead.

If I can make it there. What is wrong with her? Surly she knows this will look bad on her in court.

I lost her in the traffic and pulled up right behind Peter

at the courthouse. He was standing with two police officers.

As I got out of my car, Peter asked, "Are you okay?"

"Yes." I shook my head, walked around my car, and stared at my bashed in rear bumper.

The police took the report from me and gave Peter a copy. I walked over to a bench and sat down. Peter followed once the police were gone.

I was baffled. "What's going on? This just doesn't make any sense."

"I told Melody what happened, and she said that she believes Chloe is lashing out because she thinks she is losing. She will do anything to get the spotlight back on your flaws and away from her. She is mentally unstable and could be very dangerous." Peter sighed. "Melody would like you to come to her office after court today."

I took a deep breath and blew it out through pursed lips. "Okay."

"I think that's a good idea, Jackson. You need to get some professional help in dealing with this type of behavior, and there is no one better at the job than Melody. I know she's my wife, and I may be a little prejudiced, but I have worked with many psychiatrists and psychologists, and there just aren't any that come close to being as good at their jobs as she is."

"She is good, Peter. I like talking to her."

"Good, so please take my advice and go see her today. It will help you understand and get through court proceedings a little calmer and with a better understanding of your wife's behavior and yours, too. She can help you understand your feelings and emotions. You might be surprised to learn that most of what you're feeling is normal."

"Okay, yes, I think that would be a good idea because right now, I am very confused."

Our time in court today was short. The judge reprimanded Chloe for her actions this morning. The police had given the judge a copy of their accident report, and he let her attorney know that her actions were not tolerable. He advised the next time she tried to contact me, he would not be as lenient as he was being today; that if it happened again, she would be spending the rest of her time in jail until the trial was over.

Her attorney asked for a recess until the next morning, and the judge granted it.

CHAPTER 19

T HE SESSION with Melody started out just like the last one. I walked into her office, said good afternoon, walked over to the couch, laid down, and my mouth just didn't shut up for over an hour.

I don't know what it is about Melody, but my body relaxes, and my mind unloads when I am around her. She is so patient and kind and knows what questions to ask to get you to empty your mind.

She asked, "How are you feeling right now?" And over an hour of blabbering, I stopped answering that question.

She asked, "And how are you feeling right now?"

I scanned my body before I answered. "Relaxed and relieved."

"Good, that's a great starting point."

We talked about my wife, and Melody gave me some insight to why she is acting the way she is right now.

"You have to realize, Jackson, she's been abusing you for a long time, you just never recognized it for what it was.

"Sometimes we get so use to people's behavior we don't recognize it as being wrong. We might say to ourselves, 'it's just the way she is,' without understanding the behavior is actually abuse."

I was exhausted when I got back home. There is something about spilling your soul to someone that wipes you out. I didn't even eat dinner; I went straight to bed.

Peter called the next morning to see how I was doing.

"Great," I said. "I had a good night's sleep and feel very rested."

"Good, because we have a big day in court today."

"I'll be ready. See you at ten."

"Okay, see you there."

"There is so much going on, I just want it all to be over so I can get back to some normalcy in my life. I don't like chaos."

I don't like having my day planned by someone else.

CHAPTER 20

CHLOE'S ATTORNEY started off by verbally attacking me on the stand.

Peter kept objecting to almost every question her attorney asked. The judge must have agreed the questioning was not appropriate because on most objections, he sustained Peter and stopped the questioning.

Peter then asked me a few questions, I think, more or less to change the mood in the courtroom from hostile to calm. But then it was Peter's turn to question Chloe. He was merciless and bombarded her with questions. I could tell she was ready to explode; and she did.

"You have no right to ask me personal questions!" she screamed.

She got so emotional and loud the judge ordered a recess.

The judge then told my wife's attorney he had thirty minutes to calm her down or she would be held in contempt of court.

That's twice he's threatened her with that.

During the recess, a man came up and whispered something to Peter. I couldn't hear what he said.

Peter told me he would be right back and followed the man. He was gone almost fifteen minutes. When he returned, he was smiling.

The judge re-entered the courtroom, and the trial proceeded again.

Peter started questioning Chloe again. Whatever her attorney said to her during the recess must have worked because she was calm and answered the rest of Peter's questions, except when he asked, "Who was the man with you the night you attacked Jackson?"

She started to raise her voice, but I noticed she looked at her attorney. He was pushing his hand in a downward motion I supposed to let her know to keep her cool. She took a couple of minutes to regain her composure, but she eventually calmed.

Peter re-asked the question. "Who was the man with you the night you attacked Jackson?"

"There was no other man, and I did not attack Jackson, he attacked me," said Chloe.

Peter said, "May I remind you of Mr. Breeze's testimony on Wednesday of this week where he testified under oath that you were with a man the night the attack took place. How do you explain that?"

"He was mistaken. I do not know what he saw, but there was no one with me."

"You're positive?"

"Yes." Chloe seemed determined.

"No more questions of this witness at this time, Your Honor," said Peter.

What? How do you let her get away with lying on the stand like that?

I leaned over to say that thought to Peter when he sat down, but he turned and smiled at me.

"I have a surprise for you," he said.

"Does the defense have any more witnesses?" the judge asked Peter.

"Yes," Peter replied, "but their testimony may take some time, so I am asking for a recess for lunch, and I will call my witness when we return. If that is acceptable to you, judge."

The judge granted the lunch recess, and we went outside to the park.

"Please get some lunch and relax for a little while," said Peter. "I need to meet with someone before the trial resumes. I'll explain when I get back."

I had a lot of questions, but I let him go to his meeting. I got a couple of tacos and found a beautiful spot in the park to eat them. It was sunny, and the flowers were poking through the ground making for a peaceful lunch. It's unbelievable sometimes the peace and comfort a beautiful day can bring to the most trying situations.

WE WERE RUSHED when Peter returned, so we entered the courtroom just in time to hear the bailiff say, "All rise."

The judge asked Peter, "Are you ready to call your next witness?"

"Yes, judge, we would like to call Mr. Ross Andrews."

"NOOOO!" Chloe screamed as Mr. Andrews rose to walk toward the front of the courtroom.

I didn't know who he was; I just watched when the judge banged his gavel three times before her attorney got her to shut up—for a few minutes. But she continued screaming at Mr. Andrews as he was making his way to the witness stand.

The judge again banged his gavel and informed Chloe that she will be escorted from the courtroom if she does not control herself.

Her attorney stood, looked her in the eye, and said, "Sit down."

She complied.

Peter said, "Mr. Andrews, please state your name and occupation."

"Ross Andrews, and I am a construction foreman."

"Do you know the woman sitting at the prosecution table in this courtroom?" asked Peter.

"Yes," Mr. Andrews replied.

As I sat there, I kept getting the feeling that I knew him, but I could not figure out from where.

"What is your relationship with her," asked Peter.

"We are just friends."

"How long have you been friends?"

"Around six months."

"How did you meet her?"

"Objection," her attorney stated. "Not relevant."

The judge denied the request, so Peter asked the question again.

"How did you two meet, Mr. Andrews."

"At a bar," Mr. Andrews replied. "She came in one night all distraught. We talked and drank for a couple of hours, then I took her home."

"Do you remember what she was distraught about?" Peter asked.

"She said she had a fight with her boyfriend, and she was fed up with him."

Peter glanced at me then asked, "So, you did not know she was married?"

"No, not until all this happened. I read it in the newspaper."

"On the night in question, did you go into her apartment with her?"

"Yes, I did."

"Can you tell us what happened that night inside the apartment?" asked Peter.

"Not all of it. I only know what happened in the last few minutes we were there."

"Why only the last few minutes?" Peter questioned.

"Because she asked me to stay out in the living room until she was done, so that's what I did. But after a little while, I heard her scream."

"When you heard her scream, what did you do?"

"I ran to the bedroom and opened the door."

"What did you see when you opened the door?" Peter asked.

"A bloody mess," Mr. Andrews said. "Jackson was laying on the floor bleeding, and she was sitting on the floor holding her face and crying. I dialed 911 and told the police there was an emergency, and we needed an ambulance right away."

"And then what happened?" asked Peter.

"She jumped up and said, 'let's get out of here.'

"I told her, we cannot leave him to die, and I asked her what happened. She said he tried to kill her. She grabbed my hand and said the ambulance is on its way, they'll find him. So, we left and went to my apartment."

"And then what happened?"

"I tried to calm her down, so I could take her to the hospital, but she was so upset I could not reason with her until I told her if she didn't get help right away, her face would be permanently scarred. Then, we immediately left for the hospital.

"When we got to the hospital, the nurse and doctor asked how it happened. She told them her husband tried to kill her. They both looked at me as soon as those words came out of her mouth.

"'He is not my husband,' she said to them.

"Thankfully, I thought to myself," Mr. Andrews said. "She could have just as easily thrown me under the bus as crazy as she was acting. The nurse left the room, and I found out later that she called the police.

"The doctor told her he had called in a plastic surgeon to analyze the situation. A very short time later, the doctor returned and told her she was going into surgery immediately as soon as the surgeon was set up.

"I went over to talk to her after everyone was out of the room and she said, 'Get out of here before the police get here.'

"I told her I would stay, and she screamed for me to get out of there. So, I left. I didn't hear what she said to the police so that is the end of the story for me."

"Did you hear from her again?" asked Peter.

"Yes, three days later when she called saying she was being released from the hospital. I offered to pick her up, but she told me not to."

"Did she come over after she was released from the hospital?" Peter asked.

"No, I didn't hear from her for over two weeks. She called out of the blue and said she needed to talk to me because her husband had been charged with attempted murder.

"I said, you're joking? But she told me she had a court date in two weeks. That it was a hearing before a judge where he tried to kill her."

"Were you aware he had been stabbed?" asked Peter.

"No, I wasn't. I told her I was busy that night, but I would call her the next day. I needed to think about what she just told me. I wondered how was he charged with attempted murder? I figured something else happen that I did not know about."

"When did you talk to her again?"

"Not until the next evening. She tried to call me several times during the day, but I was working, and didn't answer my phone. I couldn't put my finger on it, but something was definitely not right.

"When she called about six, I answered the phone, and she was furious. She wanted to know where I had been and why I hadn't called her. I told her I'd been working all day and just got home."

"What did she say she wanted?" asked Peter.

"She told me we needed to talk about what happened the other night that we had to get our stories straight. I asked her about what, and she said the night I went to her apartment with her. She said she hadn't told the police about me. I wondered why she would tell them she was alone, when she could have told them I was there and have a witness.

"She screamed at me that he tried to kill her and that she didn't want anyone complicating the matter by being involved."

Mr. Andrews took a deep breath and then sighed. "I hung up the phone, and that was the last time I talked to her or seen her until today."

Peter asked him, "Did she know that I contacted you?"

"No, you asked me not to say anything to anyone, so I didn't."

Peter said he had no more questions, and the judge recessed for lunch. Chloe's attorney asked the judge if we could recess for the day, so he could get ready for cross-examination of the new witness.

The judge granted his request, so we were done for the day.

CHAPTER 22

THE NEXT DAY in court, her attorney asked Mr. Andrews just one question, "Did you see anything that happened in the apartment that night? I mean personally with your own two eyes?"

"No," Mr. Andrews responded. "I just saw the aftermath of the situation."

"Thank you," her attorney stated. "No further questions, Your Honor."

And with that one question, it was all over. The only thing that happened after that was closing arguments between both lawyers. Then court was adjourned.

It was kind of strange, almost eerie. I wasn't sure what had actually happened, but I could tell it was very powerful. It was like with one question her attorney settled everything in the mind of the judge.

Peter just sat there thinking until I asked, "What just happened?"

"Well, the judge will take his time going over all the testimony and evidence. Then he will call us all back to court and give us his decision."

"No, I'm not talking about that. What happened with her attorney only asking one question?"

"Brilliant move on his part," Peter said. "He left everyone thinking it was over. There was so much uncertainty up to that point, but after his question, it shifted the projection of the judge. The decision, though, has to be beyond a reasonable doubt. So don't worry," Peter explained.

Mr. Andrews walked over to our table and held out his hand to shake mine. "I'm sorry you're going through this, Jackson."

"Thank you, and thanks for your testimony. We really appreciate you coming forward with the information. I know it helped."

"How long before we get a verdict?" he asked.

I shrugged and looked at Peter. "I don't know."

Peter said, "It will be at least two days so go enjoy yourself."

I left the courtroom a little distraught because I wasn't feeling very good about how it ended. But I couldn't do anything about it, so I stopped at Brutas' Burger stand, ate lunch, then went to work, where everyone wanted to know what happened in court. I didn't feel like talking about it, so I just said we are waiting on a verdict.

"Good luck," everyone shouted.

I went through my inbox and sorted my emails. I had only been there about three hours when Peter called and said he needed me to come back to court right away.

"I thought you said it would be at least two days," I questioned.

"I did say that, but I need you to come right now. The judge says he's ready with his verdict, and there has been a new development in your case."

"Okay, I will be right there."

I told my boss the verdict was in, and I needed to go back to court. He said he was going with me if I didn't mind. I told him I would meet him there.

CHAPTER 23

WHEN I ARRIVED, Peter was already seated in the court-room. I sat down next to him. "What's going on? How did he make his decision that fast?"

Peter raised his eyebrows. "We're about to find out."

Then things got a little complicated, at least to me. Two police officers came in and sat down behind us. A gentleman in a Dior suit came up to Peter and whispered something to him. Peter took an envelope out of his briefcase and gave it to the man.

I leaned over to Peter. "I don't know why, but all of a sudden, I'm extremely nervous."

"I just want to warn you that things may get a little hectic and stressful for a bit, but don't panic. I have everything under control. I'll take care of you and any issues that come up."

I stared at him. "What are you talking about?"

About that time, the bailiff asked everyone to rise, and the judge made his way to his bench.

We barely sat down, when the judge asked me to stand, so I did.

The judge started talking and said he had weighed all the evidence and had a lot of options to use but wanted to be as fair as possible, given the situation.

"I have dropped the attempted murder charge and have decided since you do not have any other criminal activity on record, to charge you with attempted manslaughter. You will serve four years in the Crawford Corrections facility with the possibility of parole in two years," the judge stated almost matter-of-factly.

My heart started pounding in my chest and sweat rolled down my face. Peter put his hand on my back and tapped it lightly.

The judge ordered the officers sitting behind us to take me into custody.

One of them put the handcuffs on me, when Peter leaned in and said, "Don't panic. It'll be all right. You're not going to prison."

I wanted to believe him, but I was having a hard time getting the judge's words out of my head. "Manslaughter; four years in prison." Four years of my life gone for something I didn't do.

The police escorted me out of the courtroom, to the jail, and to my cell. They locked the door. I felt helpless, and I started to cry. That's what I did for the next hour.

A little later, Melody came in. The guard let her into the cell where I was still crying. She hugged me and told me everything was going to be okay.

"How can you say that?" I was not convinced.

"Jackson, Peter has something in the works. He didn't

have time to tell me what it was, but he wanted me to come and be with you until it is all over."

"What's all over? It was over when the judge found me guilty of manslaughter."

"Evidently not. Peter wouldn't have me come down here to be with you if he wasn't expecting something to happen to help your case."

CHAPTER 24

I STARTED FEELING a little better after Melody and I talked for a while. I noticed again there is something about Melody that makes me relax and spill all my fears and problems at the same time. It's like she puts a spell on me. I open up, tell her everything that is in my head, and then I relax and want to take a nap.

I guess she could see I was getting tired, so she told me to lay down on the cot, and she would stay and do some work on her laptop while I rested. When I woke, Melody was on the phone and still working on her computer.

"What time is it," I asked.

She looked up. "Three forty-five."

I had been sleeping for an hour and a half. "Have you heard anything from Peter."

"No, but please don't worry. Have faith in him. He is a great lawyer and knows what he is doing."

"I know he is, but what could he possibly do once the verdict has been handed down?"

"I don't know. I just know Peter, and if he told you he would take care of everything, then he will."

I sighed and plopped back down on the cot.

About thirty minutes later, the guard came in and unlocked the cell door. He took the handcuffs off and said I was free to go.

I couldn't believe it. I looked at Melody who just shrugged her shoulders. I picked up my wallet and keys at the desk and walked outside with Melody.

Her phone pinged, and I watched her reaction.

"Peter wants you to go home, and he'll be over to explain. How about I give you a ride, and we can come back and get your car later?"

"If you could just take me to my car. I would like to drive it home in case I need it."

"Okay, let's get out of here."

I followed her to her car.

Traffic was terrible, so it took us twice as long to get to my car as it normally would.

Melody said they would be over later, so I drove home, laid down, and slept for two more hours. I did not turn the TV on, I just slept.

CHAPTER 25

THE DOORBELL RANG and I jumped up.

I opened the door to Melody and Peter. They were very happy, laughing, and talking.

"What's going on."

"I came to tell you that you are a free man. All charges have been dropped." Peter grinned.

"How did all that happen when the judge just this morning sentenced me to four years in prison? I can't pretend I'm not confused."

"Well, to start with, the judge has been relieved of his duties, permanently. Also, he will probably lose his license to practice law."

"Why?" I must have looked shocked because Peter laughed.

"Mr. Andrews."

"What does he have to do with it?"

"Everything. How about a glass of wine to celebrate?"

Melody opened the wine they had brought with them, and Peter continued.

"Do you remember the day in court when I said it just

doesn't make sense that the judge doesn't seem like he is hearing what we are proving?" Peter asked.

"Yes, it was the same day that Mr. Andrews testified."

"Yes, you and I went out to the park and ate our sandwiches from the food truck."

"Yes, okay?"

"Well, Mr. Andrews went to get lunch, also, but he was parked down the street. As he was walking toward his truck, he saw a little bar and decided to stop in for lunch. I guess he walked to the end of the bar and ordered his lunch. While waiting, he was looking around the room and thought he saw your wife with another man. At first, he was going over to confront her but then decided against it. It was then he saw who she was with. He videotaped them instead without them realizing it because they were so engrossed with each other. He recorded quite a show." Peter laughed.

"Where is this going?" I looked from Peter to Melody and back again.

"According to Mr. Andrews, the two were kissing and feeling each other so hot and heavy he thought they were going to have sex right in the booth. Your wife even ended up under the table at one point. Once Mr. Andrews finished the video, he retrieved his lunch, left the bar, and called me." Peter was enjoying this, and now he burst out laughing. "Jackson, the person she was kissing and groping was the judge."

"No way." I couldn't believe it.

"Yes. Somehow, she managed to get to the judge and start a relationship with him and kept it going the entire time the trial was going on. Mr. Andrews gave me the video. I had to find trustworthy people to show it to, and when I did, they were appalled with the entire scene. They helped me find a prosecutor and judge that would overturn the conviction because of the inappropriateness of their affair."

"I can't believe it. Thank you so much, Peter."

"You're very welcome, but it was Mr. Andrews that made it happen. He didn't have to give us the video. He could have just ignored it and walked out of the bar, but he didn't. He took the time to get us a piece of information that showed the judge was bias."

"Do you know where I can find Mr. Andrews or a phone number for him so I can thank him?"

"I do have a phone number, but if you don't mind, I'll check with him first before I give it out."

"Oh sure, I understand.

"How about you call him, Peter, and give him my number and tell him I would like to speak to him. That way if he doesn't want anything to do with me, he won't feel obligated to call."

"That works."

"What is going to happen to Chloe? Is she going to continue to use people without paying the consequences?"

"I'm not sure what will happen to her yet."

"I just want to get a divorce without her trying to kill me again."

"If you would like, I can handle your divorce, and I'll get a restraining order against her. That way, if she even comes close to you, she will be arrested."

"You mean if she hasn't killed me before the police get there?" I said jokingly, but I don't think I was joking at all.

The next morning as I was fixing my coffee, my phone rang. I didn't know the number that was calling me, so I hesitated, then decided to answer. It was Mr. Andrews.

"Peter said you wanted to talk to me."

"Yes, I wanted to thank you for taking the time to record the video and deliver it to Peter. I'm sure what you did is what is keeping me from being in prison right now."

"You're welcome, but I also owe you."

"What do you mean?"

"I have learned a lot about myself and other people throughout this whole process for which I'm very grateful to you. I've learned about liars, cheaters, and that I let people use me. Even though I know he should have excused himself from the trial, I understand how the judge got caught up in her web. She is very convincing and sexy, and she uses those traits to control other people." He paused for a second. "I think I need a therapist."

"I know a good one, and she's very good at her job," I told him.

"Great, what's her name?"

"Melody, Peter's wife."

"Really? I'll give her a call."

"Yeah, you'll like her. Thanks again, Mr. Andrews. If you ever need anything, please call me."

"I will, same to you. I'm available to talk anytime. We could go have a beer or a glass of wine some night if you would like to," he said.

I smiled. "Maybe we can. Have a good night."

# CHAPTER 26

A FEW MONTHS LATER, I was sitting in the middle of the bus when it pulled up to its next stop. I looked out the window in time to see a man grab a woman by the hair and slam her against the wall. It was Celeste, from Art Therapy.

I jumped up and ran out the door of the bus, crowding past people who were trying to get on. I took a deep breath to calm myself before I reached the man and Celeste.

"Is something wrong here?" I asked.

"Mind your own business." The man snapped at me.

A police officer walked around the corner, and I yelled to get his attention.

The man told Celeste, "We'll finish this when we get home," and then he took off running.

The police offer was walking toward us. "Are you okay," I asked Celeste. Celeste was crying, and the officer also asked if she was okay.

Celeste was looking down; it was obvious she was embarrassed. "I'm fine."

"No, she's not fine. That man grabbed her by her hair and slammed her up against the wall!"

Celeste turned her head, so the officer could see the blood running from her head and down her face.

"No, I don't think you are okay," said the officer. "You probably need stitches. It's a pretty nasty cut."

"I can't go to the hospital," she said quietly. "I don't have any money or insurance."

"You cannot go around with a gash in your head and blood going everywhere. You're going to the hospital right now," the officer said.

Celeste started crying again.

I told her, "I'll go with you to help in any way I can."

She nodded briefly. "Okay."

The officer had us get in the cruiser and took us to the hospital.

When we arrived at the hospital, Celeste said, "I don't feel so good."

The officer pulled up to the emergency entrance and ran in to get help.

I jumped out and opened the car door.

An orderly came out with a wheelchair. As Celeste was getting out of the cruiser, she fainted.

I caught her before she hit the ground, and I picked her up and carried her into the hospital.

A nurse led us to a cot by the nurses' station, and the orderly pushed her back to an empty exam room. The officer sat down at a desk next to the nurse and filled out paperwork.

"How long will it be before we know anything?" I asked.

"Don't know," the officer responded. "They'll likely run some tests and sew her up. It could take a little while. Do you happen to know her name?"

"Celeste, but I don't know her last name."

An hour had passed when the doctor came out and said Celeste had a severe concussion, and that she required twenty-one stitches. She also had several other bruises.

The doctor told the police officer that he believes she is being abused, and not just today. This has been happening, according to the evidence found on her body, for a long period of time.

"We'll be keeping her for a few days for medical reasons, but I will also contact Melody Sabastin to get her involved. She can evaluate Celeste and hopefully help her mentally. But right now, we'll take care of her physical injuries," the doctor explained.

The officer finished his report with the information the doctor had given him and said he would be back the next day to talk to Celeste.

I, for some reason, felt the need to stay with Celeste. I grabbed a Snickers bar from the vending machine and settled in a chair.

A couple of hours later, the doctor came out to let me know they had run multiple tests and were waiting on results, but Celeste was sleeping comfortably now, so I could go home if I wanted because she would probably sleep the rest of the night.

"She has severe injuries, and it's going to take time to heal," said the doctor.

"Is it all right if I come back to check on her in the morning before I go to work?"

"Of course, that will be fine."

CHAPTER 27

WHEN I GOT HOME, I just couldn't relax. I remembered all the things Melody had said in her lectures about noticing signs of abuse, but this was way beyond noticing. I actually saw the man slam her head against a brick wall while pulling her hair.

But do I have the right to tell anyone?

I didn't think too long before I called Melody and gave her all the details about Celeste and the attack and the hospital where I left her. She was very appreciative and said she would take it from there.

Melody thanked me and suggested I may have prevented more serious injuries by intervening in the issue.

I felt better after talking to her, so I was able to relax and then sleep.

The next morning when I woke up, the first thing I thought about was that it was a good thing I told Melody about Celeste. The fact that she is on the staff at both hospitals in town, it will be normal for her to stop in and check on Celeste. I felt really good about telling Melody.

When I arrived at the hospital, Celeste was eating

breakfast. She had a large bandage on her head, and her arm was in a sling.

I knocked lightly on the door and walked into her room. "You look like you have been in an accident."

Celeste smiled and took another sip of her coffee.

"How are you feeling."

"Very sore, but Dr. Sabastin came to see me last night and told me not to worry because she would help me through all the difficulties I am facing. She said she would be back this morning, and we would talk more. I felt very good talking to her."

I just smiled without commenting. I don't think Celeste realizes we had met once before.

I visited for a few minutes, and then left for work telling Celeste I would be back later.

I know there is a patient/doctor confidentiality law, but I was dying to know what Melody had found out. I stopped by her office after work, but she was with a patient, so I went on to the hospital. Celeste was asleep when I arrived, so I just sat in a chair and answered emails on my phone.

A nurse came in the room shortly after I sat down.

"How is she doing," I asked.

"She's had a rough day, but that is normal for patients who have suffered abused," the nurse said.

"What do you mean?"

"These patients usually get depressed because they have put up with it so long it has become normal for them. So, when someone else starts taking care of them, in this case the hospital staff, they start to feel guilty for not feeling bad, if that makes any sense to you."

It did make sense to me, so I just nodded as she continued.

"Dr. Melody Sabastin has been with her a good part of the day, so it's been a little overwhelming for her to face the fact that what she has been through is not the norm. Abused people make excuses for the abuser because they mistake their attentiveness for love, which is not true, it's just manipulation."

Obviously, the nurse didn't know just how much I did know what Celeste was going through. Melody was still helping me work through my emotions and beliefs about abuse.

A woman rattling dinner trays woke Celeste. She seemed surprised to see me but glad, I think. She must have because she scarfed down the food like it was the best she had ever eaten. Not too many people get excited about hospital food, but she seemed to like it.

We visited for a while, and around seven forty-five, I decided to leave.

She seemed disappointed. "Do you have to go?"

"Visiting hours are almost over, so I should probably go, but I'll stop by tomorrow."

She seemed to like being in the hospital room, I surmised. She kept fluffing her pillows and straightening the blankets and sheets.

I left thinking I really wanted to talk to Melody, but I knew she may not share any information with me.

I headed home, ate some fruit and toast, then went to bed.

CHAPTER 28

WHEN I STOPPED at the hospital the next morning, Celeste was gone. I was told Melody had her, and it would probably be a while before she would be back in her room.

"Just tell her I was here," I requested.

"Of course," the nurse replied.

When I got to work, I called and set up an appointment to see Melody. I figured that was the only way I would be able to get any concrete information about Celeste.

That afternoon at three o'clock I was at Melody's office in the waiting room. When I walked into her office, she was smiling at me.

"What?" I asked.

"Are you here for you or Celeste?"

I smiled wryly. "Both. I know there's a lot you can't tell me, but what's going on with her?"

"Well, physically, she has a severe concussion. The doctors say her brain is swollen from the blow to her head. He must have really slammed her hard to do that much damage. But the marks on the rest of her body suggest repeated abuse. You probably saved her life by stepping in. That was very brave of you."

"I couldn't just stand by and let her be attacked like that. I had to do something."

"You could have been hurt yourself had the police not shown up when they did."

"I hadn't thought about that. Does she know the guy?"

"Yes, it's her boyfriend. She said it was her fault because she packed her lunch, and he said she took all the food out of the house, so he was mad at her and was going to teach her a lesson. According to her, he didn't mean to hurt her so badly. That is a typical response from someone that mistakes abuse for love. Usually, they can't separate their feelings. Even though they get hurt, they know eventually the abuser will want sex, or dinner, or some other thing where they will act kindly or lovingly toward the person that they abused, and that is what the abused is waiting on, to feel loved again."

Melody stopped and seemed to be studying me or waiting for my response. I didn't say anything.

She continued, "Unless they get therapy, it's a continuous cycle which usually ends with someone being seriously hurt, or even killed. But we know about that, don't we?"

I nodded.

"So, when I said you probably saved her life, I was not joking. The important thing right now is to keep her in therapy as long as we can, at least until we can get her to see she doesn't have to live like that. She can have a normal, healthy life without being abused. The good part, if there is a good part, about the severity of her injuries, is keeping her in the hospital and away from him. Good for me, too, because I can work with her several times a day to get her started on recovery."

"Do you know if they arrested him?"

"I don't, but hopefully, he doesn't know or doesn't care where she is right now, so he is not around to tell her therapy is a waste of time or worse yet, take her out of the hospital before she is healthy enough to leave."

"Do you think she is a good candidate for our therapy group again? I know she came that one time, but she didn't like the fact I was in the group, so she never came back."

"It isn't you that she doesn't like, it's men in general because she relates it to the abuse she is receiving."

"I guess that is why I'm a little confused, because when I was at the hospital with her, she didn't want me to leave."

"In answer to your question about being a good candidate for your group, it depends on how quickly she realizes that there are better alternatives to her lifestyle of choice right now, and that there is help available. Getting an abused victim to believe others are willing to help them without wanting something in return is a big hurdle to get over. They are used to putting up with abuse when someone comes along that pays attention to them. We'll have to see how things play out before we can make that determination."

"Do you know if she has any family?"

"I haven't gotten that far with her yet. However, I do get a good feeling about her now compared to the first time she was referred to me, and my feelings are usually on point. I figure I have a few more days while she is in the hospital to work with her which is in our favor. Getting through fear is our biggest obstacle with anyone.

"Now about you, how are you doing?"

"Pretty good. Most of the time I am great, but every once in a while, the blues come over me for no reason."

"Give yourself a break. It hasn't been that long ago since you were going through the same things."

"I know, but how long before I just forget it all."

"You probably will never forget it all. You will learn from it while you are helping others. It keeps getting easier over time, but trauma is hard to get over completely. You just move on with your life, and as you learn there are great, kind, respectful people in the world to help you, you start to realize you don't have to stay in abusive relationships any longer. At that point, your anger usually turns to pity for the abuser. Life then becomes good for you and for the people you help along the way. Sharing your story helps others see they are not alone."

"Has Celeste shared her story with you?"

"I gave you all the information I can. I will keep working with her while she is in the hospital, and hopefully, she will have a breakthrough in her mentality where she will want to continue therapy after she is discharged. She needs to get away from her boyfriend before he kills her."

CHAPTER 29

MELODY SABASTIN sat next to Celeste's hospital bed. "Celeste, you should think about taking art classes or go to school and get your degree in art, and maybe teach. I examined the work you did in the one Art Therapy class you attended; it was really nice."

Celeste shrugged. "It's just a release, something to keep my mind off other things. It really doesn't amount to much, and I can only draw when my boyfriend is not around. He says it is childish and a waste of time."

"You can continue to listen to someone that belittles you, Celeste, or you can take your life back by believing in yourself and taking strides in bettering your living situation. You have the control, don't give it to anyone else."

"How do I do that?"

"First, get a real job doing something you love."

"Like what?"

"Well, what do you like to do?"

"I love to draw. I love being outdoors especially when the sun is shining, and the birds are singing. It just makes me happy. I love taking a walk, window shopping, getting a soft chocolate ice cream cone and eating it in the park. I love a lot of things but getting to do them is a different story. I would love to have a job working with nice people, but that probably won't happen."

"Why would you say that?"

"Don't know." Celeste clammed up after that.

Melody knew not to push it at this point, so she told Celeste she would see her tomorrow and handed her a business card with a phone number. She told Celeste if she was interested in a good job with nice people, to call the number on the card and set up an interview.

A few days later after Celeste was discharged from the hospital, she met Melody at her office for her first therapy session in the office.

Melody asked her, "How are things going? Did you consider the job?"

Celeste smiled. "Yes, I have an interview tomorrow. What should I wear?"

"You should dress for success. Do you have any nice business attire."

"I do not have anything like that."

Melody stood. "I can help with that, follow me."

She led Celeste to a closet in the back room, and when she opened the door, Celeste was visibly taken back at all the nice clothes hanging in front of her. There was even underwear and coats.

Melody explained, "The Domestic Violence Women's Shelter collects the clothing for women that need proper clothing for job interviews. Try some on, Celeste. The dressing room and bathroom are through the door behind you and take as long as you like."

Celeste came out about twenty minutes later with a couple of outfits in her hand and some panties and bras.

"Dr. Sabastin, which one do you think is best?"

"Take both of them. You may need both if you see the possibility of getting the job. We have great expectations for you! If you need any more, please let me know, and you can come back and get additional outfits until you have money to buy your own clothes."

"I don't know how to thank you, Doctor."

Melody laughed. "Get the job!"

I asked Celeste if I could take her to dinner after the interview, and she agreed. When I picked her up, she was so excited. She kept talking about how nice the people were and the possibility of getting the job. We had a great evening celebrating her getting out of the hospital and her job interview.

It was about eight o'clock when I dropped her off at her apartment. I asked her if she would be safe going home alone, and she said she was okay.

She had called the apartment phone number several times that day, and no one was there, so she felt comfortable going home.

I went home, took a shower, and got into my bed feeling good that I had helped someone.

MY PHONE RINGING woke me up at midnight. I answered to hear Celeste screaming in a panic, "He's here he's here!" and then I heard a man say, "I'm going to kill you."

Then the phone went dead.

I immediately called Melody and told her what I had heard.

"I'll take care of it," said Melody.

I started to get dressed. "I'm on my way."

"Stay where you are, Jackson."

"No, I want to help her." I hung up the phone.

Melody raced out the door telling Peter what was happening. "Call the police, Peter. The address is on the nightstand beside you."

She knew that the man could very well kill someone because abusers don't think, they just react to their own anger.

Melody was first to arrive at Celeste's apartment.

She knocked on the door; no one answered, so she banged on the door and screamed for Celeste.

The lock clicked, and the door flew open. Celeste stood there; her face was covered with blood.

Celeste shouted, "Go away."

But before Melody could respond, a man grabbed her by the hair and dragged her into the apartment.

Celeste tried to fight him, but he backhanded her across the mouth.

"Don't hurt her!" Celeste screamed as he shoved Melody to the floor.

When I got there, I banged on the door.

Celeste's boyfriend opened the door.

I pushed my way in. "What's going on in here? Are we having a party tonight?"

Melody yelled, "Jackson, run!"

The boyfriend slugged Melody with his fist and knocked her out, then he put Celeste in a headlock, dragged her to the door, and locked it.

"Oh, it's the new boyfriend," he snarled. "Get over in the corner where I can see you or I will snap her neck," he told me.

I knew he wasn't joking. I started toward the corner but instead went to Melody who was on the floor.

She wasn't moving and I was scared. I didn't know if she was dead, but then I noticed she was still breathing.

The boyfriend yelled, "I told you to get in the corner!"

He still had Celeste in a headlock, and I didn't want him to hurt her again, so I did and sat on the floor. I needed to do something. But what?

I knew I had to be careful, but doing nothing wasn't helping at all.

Relief rushed over me when I heard sirens, and I was hoping they were headed this way.

"Sit there and shut up." The boyfriend looked around anxiously.

"What are you planning to do with us?" The sirens got louder.

"I told you to sit there and shut up, and I won't tell you again."

He turned his back on me, and I lunged toward him and slammed him in the back. We both fell to the floor, and now Celeste was free from his grasp.

"Get out of here!" I yelled.

Celeste scrambled down the hall back to the living room.

I heard banging on the door, and then someone yelled, "Police! Open up!"

The man jumped up, and I grabbed his leg, but he kicked me in the head with his other foot, knocked me to the floor, and stomped on my head.

Celeste tried to unlock the door when her boyfriend pulled her hair and drug her back to the bedroom.

The police kicked the door down. They entered cautiously. One of the officers hurried over to Melody lying on the floor.

Celeste was still screaming, and they stepped over me going toward the back of the apartment.

When the police reached Celeste, her boyfriend had a gun pointed at her temple.

He yelled at them, "Stop! Or I'll kill her!"

"Okay, okay, I'm Sergeant Lane, just stay calm and put the gun down."

"Get out!" the boyfriend yelled again.

Sergeant Lane motioned for the rest of his staff to back off.

They retreated to the living room to help me and Melody; we were both still lying on the floor, and I couldn't move. I could hear everything that was being said, but my body was paralyzed. I didn't know if it was from fear or if something terrible was happening to me.

The EMTs were putting Melody on a backboard ready to take her to the hospital when Peter came flying through the door. He saw the blood on Melody and went crazy. He ran back to the room where I could hear Sergeant Lane was trying to talk Celeste's boyfriend into putting the gun down.

Before Peter got to Sergeant Lane, he stopped and backed off.

Peter saw Sergeant Lane put his gun away.

As soon as he did, Celeste's boyfriend jumped on top of Sergeant Lane, and then a gun went off.

The rest of the police force ran back down the hall.

Everyone stopped.

No more screaming, no more shouting, just quiet.

Celeste screamed and went into an all-out panic attack. She was on the floor crying so hard she was shaking and couldn't catch her breath.

The medic couldn't control her and called for help.

The police rolled the body of Celeste's boyfriend off Sergeant Lane.

One of the officer's asked him, "Are you all right?"

The sergeant was covered in blood, and even though he thought he was okay, he wasn't sure. He didn't know if he had been hit by the bullet or not.

More medics arrived and were able to subdue Celeste enough to take her to the hospital.

Celeste's boyfriend was dead. Shot in the back of the head.

The police taped off the apartment and called in the investigators to complete the reports and collect evidence, and they convinced me to go to the hospital with the ambulance that was taking Melody.

I arrived at the hospital first, and the doctors had me in surgery within thirty minutes.

According to Peter, Melody was run through a battery of tests, and it was determined that she had no broken bones, but her body was badly bruised. The doctors decided to admit her to the hospital for overnight observation.

Peter told me he was relieved when Melody opened her eyes and spoke to him. "She had a severe headache, so after all the tests were completed, they put her in a room for the night. They gave her pain medication. It didn't take long for it to work. She was asleep within fifteen minutes of taking the meds.

"I just laid my head on the bed next to her body. I couldn't get myself to leave even though the nurse told me she would be monitored closely all night. I was so grateful just to be with her," Peter added.

I was told I would have to have surgery on my broken jaw. Even though I had recovered from my previous surgeries caused by my now ex-wife, the new injuries caused a lot of trauma to my body. When I got out of surgery, they put me in ICU for precautionary measures.

CHAPTER 31

CELESTE

I WENT TO THE HOSPITAL the next morning to check on Jackson, but they would not let me in the ICU.

The nurse informed me, "Family only at this time."

I went to the waiting room and just sat there. A couple of hours later, Peter walked in, he said hi, then went to get a cup of coffee.

I guess he realized who I was, and he asked, "How are you doing?"

"I'm actually fine, but they won't let me in to see how Jackson is doing."

He took a sip of his coffee then sat in a chair next to me. "Not family, right?"

I rolled my eyes. "Right. How is Melody doing?"

"They kept her last night for observation, but if all goes well today, I think she may go home later this evening. Her face is swollen and bruised, along with a black eye which is going to take a while to heal. Thankfully, she's alive, actually, that all of you are alive." He paused then continued, "I heard what you did to save everyone, and I will be forever grateful to you. I'm sorry you had to go through something that tragic, but you saved several lives last night. I also know seeing your boyfriend killed had to be hard, and I thank you from the bottom of my heart."

I took a deep breath. "Being in a relationship with him has been hard, too, but I never wished for him to die."

"No, I'm sure you didn't." Peter stood and smiled. "I'll see what I can do to get you in to see Jackson."

"Thank you."

Peter left. I don't know if he had anything to do with it, but around an hour later, the nurse let me know that she was now permitted to let people in to visit Jackson.

When I walked into the room, I immediately started to cry, and I ran to Jackson who held out his arms. I cried for several minutes before I calmed down.

I sat in the chair next to his bed, and he asked, "Are you all right?"

"He's dead, Jackson, I killed him."

"What?" Jackson looked surprised.

The doctor and nurse both came into the room.

"You need to leave for a few minutes," the nurse said to me.

"No, she doesn't," Jackson protested, but I was already starting toward the door.

The doctor was saying, "Mr. Madison, you need to calm down. Your heart is racing, and you won't be good to any-one if you have a heart attack right here in the hospital."

The nurse added, "You are in ICU for this very reason. Please relax and get some sleep."

"That will help you more than anything else to heal right now," said the doctor.

On my way out of the room, the doctor stopped Peter from coming in to see Jackson. "Let's give him a day or two before you visit."

Peter turned and followed me into the waiting room. I sank into a chair and started to cry.

"Well, guess we got told." Peter chuckled. "Are you okay? Do you need anything?"

"I told the police I can't go back to my apartment until the investigation was over, so I don't have a place to stay. I'm going to hang out here until I can talk to Jackson and Melody."

"I'll get you a room in the hotel across the street from the hospital, so you can get some rest. That way, you'll be close when the doctors say it is okay to see them."

"I appreciate it, but it's not necessary."

"You need rest, too. You've had a traumatizing day, so go rest."

Peter was right, it had been a traumatic day.

W HEN I GOT TO THE HOTEL ROOM, I laid across the bed and fell asleep. A noise in the hallway woke me up. I looked at the clock, and it was only eight p.m. I had only been asleep for an hour, so I curled up on the bed and went back to sleep.

The phone rang and woke me up again. I looked at the clock wondering who would be calling this late, but the clock said it was only nine p.m., so I answered the phone.

"Good morning," Peter said.

"Morning?" I questioned.

"Yes, you can see Melody anytime you get back to the hospital. Take your time."

"Thank you, Peter. I'll be right over."

I couldn't believe it was morning. I had slept all night for the first time in years. I couldn't remember the last time I felt this good and rested. Even though I didn't have extra clothes to put on, I jumped in the shower, but I just stood there enjoying the warm water running over my body. No one was telling me to hurry up, or not to use all the hot water.

I was no longer plagued by fear. I could stand in the shower as long as I wanted. I even smelled the soap. Such a sweet scent, I've never had a girly soap or shampoo before. I rubbed the soap all over my body enjoying the texture of how it felt as the water washed it off, and the shampoo was wonderful.

So, this is how it feels to be free.

I took a deep breath as I was drying off and just smiled. I wanted to get over to see Melody, but I just couldn't force myself to rush. I was enjoying the simplicity of life and the luxury of the hotel. I had a lot to think about now that I was alone.

After such a tragic night, how could I feel this good? Am I a bad person for feeling this happy?

I let the thought go and flopped back down on the bed again. It was wonderful to enjoy all this beauty and niceties without someone yelling at me.

Checkout was at noon, so I stayed until eleven forty-five and then took the key down to the desk.

I felt pretty again, even in clothes I had worn the day before. By the time I got to the hospital, Peter was leaving.

"I'm so sorry that I'm so late," I told him.

"Not a problem. I'm glad you got some rest. I need to run to my office right now, so I'll leave you to talk to Melody. I'll be back later. We'll need to talk."

"Okay," I agreed.

"Would three o'clock be okay?"

"Yes, that will work." I was not sure what the day held in store for me.

I went into Melody's room. She had some bruising on her face and a bandage across her forehead, but she seemed like her normal self, chipper and smiling.

"I'm so sorry I got you involved in all of this, Melody."

"If we hadn't been involved, that could have been you dead instead of your boyfriend."

I sighed. "I know you're right, but you and Jackson are in the hospital because you helped me." I looked at the floor. "I don't think Jackson is doing very well because he is still in ICU. They won't let me see him until they move him out of ICU."

"Peter is keeping in touch with Jackson's doctor. He's a friend of ours, and he's also the same doctor that treated Jackson after the tragedy with his ex-wife. So, he knows the history, and I'm sure he's being overly cautious."

"Peter said we needed to talk later. Do you know what that's about?"

"Yes, the police will have a lot of questions for you about last night. That's why Peter wanted you to stay in the hotel last night, so they wouldn't talk to you without him being present."

I felt uneasy. "Am I in trouble?"

"No, but it's an ongoing investigation involving a death, so they have to get statements from everyone. Please don't worry. Peter and I will handle everything for you."

The nurse walked in the room, and I ask her if it was possible to see Jackson.

"No one is permitted to visit in ICU, except for family."

Melody asked, "Is he doing okay?"

The nurse said, "He had a rough night."

Melody and I became very quiet. I could tell Melody was just as concerned about Jackson as I was.

They brought Melody's lunch and sat the tray on the table. I helped Melody uncover and unwrap everything and then I decided to leave.

"Where are you going?"

"I'm not sure, but you need to eat and get some rest."

"Celeste, you can go to the studio and paint if you like, the bus picks up out front of the hospital every thirty minutes. I'll call the studio and let them know you're coming if you like."

I smiled. "I may just do that."

"You should, it would do you good."

"Okay, I have to be back by three anyway, so I'll see you then."

CHAPTER 33

W HEN I ARRIVED at the studio, I felt at ease, like I was in a safe environment. Everyone there was so nice. I went back to one of the tables, got comfortable, and started sketching.

My pencil floated across the paper as if it was saying something. I felt I had no control over what I was drawing. I didn't fight it, but just went with the flow. Two hours later, I looked at the drawing and couldn't believe what I saw. The picture was a beautiful ocean landscape. Actually, unbelievable. I just stared at it.

Peter called to remind me of our meeting at three. I told him I was on my way. I took the picture and put it in one of the lockers then caught the bus back to the hospital. I went straight to Melody's room where Peter was waiting, but neither of them seemed to be in a good mood.

I was a little hesitant, but I asked, "Is everything all right?"

"No," Melody said. "Jackson is not doing well at all. The doctor says his heartbeat is very irregular, so they are keeping him in ICU for a while longer."

"So, we can't see him yet?"

"Peter can because he is the only one Jackson has asked for, so they may be assuming he is the closest family member."

"But he's not family, is he?"

"No, he's not."

"I'll try to talk to the doctor after our meeting and ask if you can see him."

"Thanks. I think I might could help him. I don't know why, but I feel that I can."

My meeting with Peter took about forty-five minutes. We were standing in the hallway when the doctor approached Peter.

Peter asked the doctor if Jackson's girlfriend could see him.

"I didn't know he had a girlfriend, who is she?"

"Celeste," Peter responded.

I was shocked that Peter suggested that I was Jackson's girlfriend.

The doctor turned to me. "You must be Celeste."

I nodded when he shook my hand. "Yes, hi."

"Where will you be?" the doctor asked me.

"Either in the waiting room or in Melody's room."

The doctor left the room, and I said to Peter, "I'm not Jackson's girlfriend."

"You are right now, at least for the time being. It's the only way I could get you into his room."

I chuckled, even feeling a little silly. "Thanks, Peter."

I went to the waiting room and sat down. I wondered what it would be like to be Jackson's girlfriend. He was so kind and tenderhearted. I thought of him touching my body in a sensual way and got goosebumps.

A nurse interrupted my dream date to tell me I could see Jackson now. I wanted to see him, but I was enjoying my imaginary date with him and didn't want it to end.

CHAPTER 34

WHEN I WALKED into Jackson's room, I was startled by all the tubes, oxygen, and equipment hooked up to him.

I sat in the chair by Jackson's bed and took his hand. He squeezed mine, but he didn't open his eyes. I sat there for the next two hours.

When the doctor came in to examine Jackson, he asked me to step out of the room for a few minutes.

"I'll let you know when I am finished," said the doctor.

I didn't go far, I wanted to be available when the doctor said I could return to his room.

About fifteen minutes later, the doctor asked me to come back into the room.

"How is he," I asked.

The doctor answered me with a question. "Would you mind if I ask you a few questions?"

"I don't know much about his family history or anything like that, but I'll answer what I can."

"How long were you with him, today?"

I looked at my watch. "Two hours."

"What did you do while you were with him?"

"I just sat by his bed and held his hand."

Peter walked into the room while the doctor was questioning me. Apparently, he had heard the previous question, so he decided he needed to be involved in the conversation.

"What's going on?" Peter asked the doctor.

"I was just asking this young lady some questions about her visit with Jackson this afternoon."

"Is there something wrong?" asked Peter.

While they were talking, I sat down next to Jackson and took his hand. Again, he squeezed my hand but didn't open his eyes.

"No, there's nothing wrong," said the doctor.

"Then why all the questions?"

"During the afternoon while Celeste was with Jackson, his blood pressure went down, his heart rate stabilized, and all his vital signs improved," said the doctor.

Then the doctor asked me, "When you held his hand, did he open his eyes?"

"No, he just squeezed my hand."

"Did he squeeze it more than once?" the doctor asked.

"Not when I was here before," I said, "but when I sat down on this chair and took his hand just now, he squeezed it again."

Peter looked curious. "Why do you ask?"

"I'm not sure, but whatever the reason, when Celeste is holding his hand, his vitals respond positively. That's the best news we have had for a couple of days. At least he's responding to touch, at least her touch, which is more than we have been able to do. It seemed like he had given up, and he was deteriorating. That is the first positive sign since his surgery."

"Ms. Celeste," the doctor said. "If it's okay with you, I will inform the hospital staff that you can visit Jackson anytime you choose. Now, when I say that he does need rest periods with no interruption so please plan accordingly."

"I understand."

"How about Melody and me?" Peter asked. "Can we still visit him?"

"Yes, of course."

Peter went back to Melody's room, and I followed him. Her doctor was just finishing up with her exam. The doctor told Peter that if Melody has another good night, he will release her in the morning.

Peter was excited and gave Melody the news about Jackson.

Maybe things are starting to get back to normal.

"Peter, would you mind taking Celeste somewhere to get a fresh change of clothes?"

A nurse who was in the room said, "There is a really cute boutique right down the street from the hospital."

"Great! Peter, would you just go and pay for her items after she picks them out?" asked Melody.

"Are you okay to go right now?" asked Peter.

I agreed to go shopping and then check back into the hotel for another night. I actually had a good time shopping for clothes. I've never had the opportunity or the money to shop at a boutique before. I tried on so many clothes, and the ladies working at the boutique were wonderful about helping me choose what looked the best. After shopping, I went back to the hotel and hung up my new clothes. I took a hot bath and soaked for a long while, then I went to bed.

Everything was looking up. I was feeling really good.

CHAPTER 35

I WAS IN A DEEP SLEEP when the hotel phone woke me up at two a.m.

I answered to hear Peter yelling, "Get to the hospital now, Jackson isn't doing well."

I dressed as quickly as I could and ran over to the hospital. When I arrived, Melody and Peter were waiting outside Jackson's room.

"What's going on?" I asked.

"The doctor said his heart rate keeps dropping, and they are afraid of losing him if it continues," said Peter.

The nurse came out and asked all of us to come into the room. We went in, and I walked over to the bed. Jackson had his eyes open, and I took his hand.

Peter and Melody watched with the doctor as Jackson's heart rate stabilized.

"Unbelievable," the doctor said. "I have never seen anyone affect a patient that way before."

Jackson squeezed my hand and smiled.

The doctor chuckled. "You're going to have to stick like glue to him until he fully recovers."

I looked directly at Jackson. "Whatever it takes."
"It may take a long while," Jackson said with a smile.
I didn't say anything. I just smiled.

CHAPTER 36

JACKSON AND CELESTE

ONCE CELESTE KNEW Jackson was going to be okay, she went back to her job during the day. Now that she was on her own, she could not afford to miss work. She talked it over with Jackson and he agreed. He knew she loved her job. It brought a new perspective to her life which she had never been allowed to use because of being abused by the people in her life.

Jackson was in the hospital a total of four weeks and then was released to go home with home health care keeping an eye on him for the next two weeks. He argued about that for some time with the doctor, but was unsuccessful, so he relinquished his argument and went along with the provisions of his discharge from the hospital.

Celeste agreed to go over every night after work to fix dinner. They had enjoyable evenings, watching TV, playing cards, or taking a walk around the neighborhood.

Jackson was getting stronger every day.

One evening on their walk, Celeste said, "They called

today to say I could go back to my apartment tomorrow."

"How do you feel about that?" asked Jackson.

"Not sure."

"I'll go with you if you would like me to."

Celeste's eyes sparkled. "I would love that. I'm not sure how I will feel when I walk back through that door, but I'm tired of living in the shelter."

"I understand. We'll go after you get off work tomorrow, then we can stop and get dinner."

"Sounds like a good plan."

Jackson grinned. "I'll pick you up tomorrow after work."

JACKSON

As we pulled up to the apartment, Celeste got a little anxious. Her breathing was quick and deep. I think she was wondering if she could go back into the apartment where Melody and I were almost killed.

I put my hand over hers. "Take a deep breath."

As we walked through the door of the apartment, Celeste had an anxiety attack. She couldn't catch her breath, so I pulled her close and held her for several minutes until she calmed.

"We can do this at another time."

"No, I want to do it now," Celeste protested.

As we walked through the rooms, I made it a point to open the closets to make sure they were clear. I was surprised to see there were pictures painted on the closet walls. Some were just black-and-white drawings, but others were bright paintings, and all of them had big black marker streaks through them, but you could still see they were well thought out and beautiful.

"Was the artwork already here when you moved into the apartment?"

"No."

"Did you do these?"

"Yes, that's why he got so mad when he found them that night when you and Melody got hurt. He blamed you because when he found the paintings, he accused me of being unfaithful to him. He said I let you trick me into sleeping with you by you telling me my artwork was good.

"No matter how I tried to explain we were not sleeping together, that I hardly knew you, and was just trying to fulfill a need inside of me by painting, like Melody suggested.

"He said I was an untalented idiot and would never amount to anything without him. He said no one like you would ever be serious about me. Then he started beating me. You saved my life that night. If you and Melody had not come over, he would have killed me. He actually said that it was what he was going to do, and then he pulled out the gun."

Celeste started sobbing so hard she could not catch her breath. I immediately took her out of the apartment and back to the car. She was trying to talk between the sobs telling me she needed to go back in.

"Not tonight. We'll come back in a few days and try again."

By the time we got back to my apartment, Celeste had regained her composure, but she was exhausted. She lay back in the recliner and fell asleep. I put a quilt over her and let her sleep thinking she would wake in a little while and go back to the women's shelter where she was staying, but three hours later, she was still asleep, so I went to bed. It was Friday night, and she didn't have to go to work the next day, so I let her sleep.

I woke the next morning, showered, shaved, and went to the kitchen and started making breakfast. Celeste was in the same spot I had left her in the night before. It wasn't until I started frying bacon that she stirred.

"Good morning," I said.

"What time is it?"

"Almost nine."

"I need to go." She started to sit up.

"Where are you going? Don't you want breakfast?"

"Breakfast? We just had dinner."

I realized she thought it was still nighttime, so I said softly, "It's morning, Celeste."

"What?" She practically jumped out of the recliner.

I laughed. "Yes, morning. Now go wash up and come and have breakfast with me."

Celeste came into to the kitchen, and we sat down to eat. We talked about the previous night and how it affected her.

"I need to go back to the apartment."

"You need to wait a few days. We'll talk to Melody before trying again."

"I have to get out of the shelter, Jackson. They've already allowed me to stay longer than they were supposed to."

"Look, I have an extra room here. Why don't you stay with me until Melody thinks you're ready to return to the apartment? You've been taking care of me over the last several weeks, it's the least I can do to repay you for your kindness."

Celeste was quiet for a few seconds. "I'll have to go get what little I have at the shelter."

She sighed. "Let me think about it for a little while."

After breakfast, she went outside for a walk.

"You want me to come with you?"

"No, I just want to walk and think for a while, okay?"

"Sure, don't mind me, I'll just be here doing the dishes."

That brought a smile.

She returned about an hour later, and she agreed to take me up on my offer.

I took her back to the bedroom she would be using. "It has its own bathroom and closets. We can get your stuff tomorrow, that way you will be all moved in by the time we go back to work Monday."

CHAPTER 38

CELESTE

I DIDN'T TELL JACKSON what I was thinking, but the reality was, I had never felt so content. The peacefulness of my life now is something I had never experienced before. Jackson was so kind and generous to me. I knew I was falling in love with him, and I didn't know how to stop myself.

We held hands everywhere we went but that was it. Maybe he was just being kind, and that was all there was to it. I fell asleep while wondering what Jackson was thinking.

At work the next day, I was so excited to get my first paycheck. Melody had gotten me the job as the receptionist at Family Services, and I was very grateful. I loved my job. I was able to give back to others the help I had received. I could let them know they would get the help they needed.

After work, I rushed home to Jackson's and started making dinner. I left my paycheck lying on the counter. When Jackson walked in, I handed it to him.

He smiled, hugged me, and said, "Good job," and then he laid the check back on the counter.

He showered and shaved, then returned to the kitchen to help finish dinner. As we finished eating, I again handed him my paycheck.

"You showed it to me already when I got home."

"No, I mean it's for you."

"I don't want your paycheck. Why would you give it to me?"

"That's what I'm supposed to do."

"What are you talking about?"

"Whenever I got paid from work, whoever I was with at the time told me I had to give them my paycheck. Then they would pay bills and get groceries. There was hardly any left for food after bills were paid."

"Well, that's not happening now."

"What am I supposed to do with it then?"

"Spend it on yourself, buy your lunch, buy new clothes, whatever you want."

"I don't even know how to cash my check. I always just signed it and turned it over."

Jackson leaned toward me. "I will teach you how to cash and deposit your check. We'll go to the bank, set up a checking account, a savings account, and get you a debit card. We'll also apply for a credit card in your name."

I started to cry uncontrollably. "Why would you do that for me?"

He lifted my chin and looked into my tear-filled eyes. "Because I love you."

THE END

For those of you that had the courage to
take your life back from abuse, I applaud you
and am very proud of you.

For those of you that still need help:
Call the **National Domestic Violence Hotline at**
800-799-7233

They are available 24 hours a day.

You can do it!

ACKNOWLEDGMENTS

I would like to thank Debbie Rasmussen for all of her expertise in editing my book. Her encouragement in helping me finish my book is much appreciated. She worked tirelessly through many days of perfecting the story and I could not have done it without her.

I appreciate all the hard work that Francine Platt put into the interior design and also her work to get the cover of the book design perfect. Thanks for all your work and time you spent with me.

And to Richard Paul Evans for the work he puts in to helping other authors succeed

To my husband Scott; Thank you for always supporting me in whatever I do. You are the light of my life.

ABOUT THE AUTHOR

C.L. CARR is a wife, mother and a grandmother. She was born and raised in Ohio and has a bachelor's degree in Business Administration. She has owned several business in the area where she lives. She loves to cook and opened a successful restaurant which was her favor-ite job of all time. She has written stories and poetry for years for her own enjoyment. This story was several years in the mak-ing before she decided to publish it. She and her husband taught Country and Western dance for ten years and she loves to go hear her son's band play so she can dance again. She and her husband will be snowbirds soon, going to Flor-ida during the winter months. Being with her husband, children and grandchildren is the joy of her life.

9 798889 454006 1